WHO'S THE MONSTER?
Classic Monsters Anthology #2

www.YeOldeDragonBooks.com

Ye Olde Dragon Books
P.O. Box 30802
Middleburg Hts., OH 44130

www.YeOldeDragonBooks.com

2OldeDragons@gmail.com

ISBN 13: 978-1-952345-82-1

Published in the United States of America
Publication Date: October 15, 2022

Table of Contents

Foreword

Lightning sizzles and crashes, as electrical charges flash across the sky.

An inhuman scream rips the darkness of the deep forest and sends you running for your life.

A castle high on a mountaintop looms ahead. Sanctuary? Perhaps, but every turret shrieks danger!

Yes, this is the second edition of *Ye Olde Dragon Books Classic Monsters Anthologies,* and we are delighted to bring you ten versions of Frankenstein as you've never seen him before. But is he the monster that Mary Shelley wrote about? Or was he the victim of a truly evil scientist, a man so deranged that *he* was truly the monster? We asked our authors to explore this concept: Who IS the monster?

You'll have to decide as you journey with each of our authors. You'll sympathize with the "monster" in a few stories, wondering at a world that would base their judgements on size and appearance alone. You'll chuckle at experiments gone amok and misplaced affection. You might even feel a chill at the thought of misplaced memories and feelings of déjà vu! Your heart will pound as you race through a haunted house with a monster at your heels. You'll probably even feel a certain chill of apprehension at a couple of stories that hit closer to home as scientists play God and try to remake men to be "better" or "stronger" with devastating results, or try to remake the past so they can reinvent the present. And yes, we even have an AI, a man, and a … virus? Who's the monster?

Whatever your reactions, I would suggest you leave the lights on tonight.

Happy reading!
Deborah Cullins Smith
September 2022

Huh? Another anthology?

Thanks for coming back, if you've adventured with us before, and trying us out, if this is your first dipping-the-toes experience with Ye Olde Dragon Books.

When Deb first proposed we do monsters in the fall and fairy tales in the spring, I was a little iffy, because monsters just aren't my "thing." But this is turning out to be kinda fun!

It's amazing and fascinating seeing all the variations of the theme of Frankenstein – doctor and monster – different imaginative people can come up with. I'm delighted to see authors returning from one anthology to the next, and new friends joining the ranks. I think you'll agree this one is creepy and kooky, mysterious and spooky ... but no ooky, please? (am I violating copyright here?) And what word means "fun" and rhymes with kooky?

Get ready for a wide variety of chills and tear-jerking, humor and "huh?" moments. Curl up with your favorite fall beverage in your comfy chair, and be prepared to leave the lights on, just in case…

Michelle L. Levigne
September 2022

MONSTER GIRL
Kaitlyn Emery

Her wails moved me. They echoed the pain embedded in my own heart.

I approached the mangled metal vehicle. There she was, pale, blood dripping down her forehead from the accident, clinging to the corpses of her parents as the warmth of their bodies drained from them. The mountain road was treacherous this time of year, and not the first time I'd witnessed black ice spin a vehicle out of control. But it was the first time I'd witnessed a survivor.

I took off the hoodie I was wearing, exposing the never-ending ropes of scars marring every inch of my skin. The doors to the vehicle were crushed, so I went in through the shattered sunroof, shards of glass cutting into my skin as I cleared a large enough opening for her to safely climb out. But first, she would have to accept my outstretched, disfigured hand.

She clung to her mother, looking down at the scars crisscrossing the back of my hand and up my arm. I waited patiently, arm outstretched. After a moment, with tears soaking her face, she glanced at her parents one last time, their expressions lifeless, and reached toward me.

I pulled her up, shaking and shivering, and wrapped her in my hoodie before helping her down.

There wasn't much I could do. I set her under the sheltering arms of a tree, shielding her from the silent falling snow. She looked so small sitting there, pulling my hoodie around her body like a blanket. I turned her face away from the vehicle as it caught fire. No child should have to watch the flames consume their loved ones, even if they were dead. At least the warmth would keep her from developing frostbite long enough for help to be drawn to the area from the rising smoke.

It was time for me to go; I had stayed too long. The best way to remain a legend was by limiting interactions with people as much as possible. I turned toward my home in the desolate forest, but her voice stopped me in my tracks.

"P-please. Don't leave me."

I winced from the terror in her voice. "You'll be all right, kid. The rangers will be here soon." I retraced my steps, zipping up the oversized black hoodie and pulling the hood over her blond curls. "Just pretend like I wasn't here. It's better for everybody that way."

"P-please," she stuttered. "I'm scared."

I could see the whites of her eyes as she gripped my shirt, pulling me toward her. Gently, I placed my hand over her fist, encouraging her to release her grip. "You're gonna be okay, little one."

I could see headlights glowing at the top of the hill off in the distance. I had to leave. Now. Closing my eyes, I put physical distance between us.

"Sorry, kid. I really gotta go. But help is on its way."

I quickly darted into the woods, her cries following me. She would be fine, I assured myself. As fine as a kid who was the only survivor of a terrible accident could be. This would be just one more memory to flood my mind and drown me in its endless echo.

Mortality was, at best, insanity.

~~~~~

"Hey, earth to monster girl!"

A crumpled piece of paper hit the side of my head, causing me to break my focus on the computer screen in front of me.

"I swear, if you do that again, I will sneeze on your glasses, Lincoln." I swiveled my rolling chair around to face him.

Lincoln flinched and threw up his hands to protect his eyewear. "No, don't!"

I scoffed before turning back to the computer I was fixing.

"Sheesh, why you gotta be so violent?" Lincoln asked, letting down his guard and sticking his hand back into his Cheetos bag.

"Why do you have to be so annoying?"

"Hurtful!"

I smiled, putting the last screw in place. "Done."

"Seriously? You're a lifesaver, Kat!"

Chuckling, I started packing up my equipment from his college dorm room. "You need more of a life, Lincoln."

He cleaned the Cheetos dust off his hands and caressed the smooth surface of the laptop. "Nah, I've got you and Delilah."

"You know it's super nerdy to name your computer, right? Only furthering my point that you need more of a life. This isn't high school anymore. No one's giving us swirlies for existing."

"Speak for yourself. The guy at the end of my dorm keeps giving me the stink eye. I'm pretty sure he wants to fight me."

"He probably just wants your bag of Cheetos," I said with a shrug. I snagged a couple, popping them into my mouth, and wiped my hand on my jeans. "Anyways, I gotta go."

"Wait, what? I thought you were gonna stay and hang out?"

"Not tonight. I'm heading out."

"Out to where? You're not going camping tonight, are you? We've got that big storm coming in."
~~~~~

"Not camping, just a hike."

Lincoln rolled his eyes. "Just a hike. You say that like it's just a stroll in the park! Your version of hiking is hours of new trail explora—"

I placed my hand over Lincoln's mouth, blocking whatever else he planned on saying. "I'll make sure I'm back in plenty of time. It's just a quick trip to clear my head."

Lincoln pulled my hand off. "It's never quick with you. I know, I've been dragged along on your monster hunting expeditions."

"No monster hunt this time, promise," I replied, making a big invisible x over my heart for extra emphasis.

"Yeah, whatever. Go look for Bigfoot."

I smiled, giving Lincoln a quick squeeze. "You're the best friend anyone could ask for!"

"I'm your only friend, Kat."

"Aww, and I'm yours, how cute!" I teased, using the toe of my Converse to nudge his foot before slinging my bookbag onto my shoulder. "Still on for breakfast tomorrow?"

"I'll be there."

"Perfect. See ya later!"

"Thanks again for helping me out, Kat. I owe you," Lincoln said as he followed me to the door.

"I know. How would you live without being able to play your World of Warcraft?"

"Hey, I don't tease you about your oddities," he complained.

I cocked an eyebrow. "Yeah, you do, that's why we work. We're both weird. But you're right, you do owe me, so next time I need someone to check on Fat Louie while I'm out camping, you're my first call."

Lincoln groaned. "You know I hate cats."

"Take some extra allergy meds and you'll be fine," I said over my shoulder as I headed into the dorm hallway. "Or you could just come with me next time and bring your camera. We could make a documentary or something while we're out there."

"Oh no, I'm not doing that again! The last time you almost killed me, and I got poison ivy in…" Lincoln glance down both sides of the hallway, before lowering his voice. "Unmentionable places."

I laughed. "Yeah, okay, fine. No camping for you. See ya later, Lincoln." Without waiting for more of his concern, I headed down the hall and out to my car.

Living on the edge of a mountain range covered in dense forestry meant it wasn't far to get to where I was going. People thought I was crazy. Except Lincoln. And maybe my therapist? Although, come to think of it, my therapist found my obsession with searching the woods to be unhealthy, so she probably thought I was crazy, too.

I parked my car at the base of the hiking trails, pulling a map with all sorts of red scribbles on it out of my glovebox. I wanted to explore Devil's Pass some more but wasn't sure I could make it far enough along the trail before dark.

Glancing at my watch, I decided I'd be fine.

Shedding my coat, I grabbed the hiking pack and survival kit out of the trunk of my beat-up car and pulled my hoodie on. It was oversized — not meant for my small frame — and worn thin. Lifting the corner of the black fabric up to my nose, I inhaled deeply, memories flooding my senses.

This ragged piece of fabric was my one piece of sanity from that fateful night that had changed my life forever. Everyone told me one of the park rangers must have given it to me and I just forgot, but I could vividly see the man's face, his dual-colored eyes, the scars on his body, and his tenderness when he pulled me out of the wreckage before it caught fire. I remembered him shielding me from the glass shards as he pulled me out of the sunroof, cutting his own body in the process. I could remember the gentle pat on my head as he pulled the hood over my then-blond curls. And I remembered him telling me help was coming.

I hit the trails, the heaviness of my backpack helping to ground me.

Maybe my therapist was right? People had tried to tell me the trauma I experienced led my brain to concoct a story that made more sense at the time. But that still didn't explain the hoodie.

I had spent years being passed back and forth from foster home to foster home. Some of them were nice. Others were not. But an eight-year-old's success story in the system was almost as rare as me finding my mysterious savior.

I was labeled a runaway, which was fair since I was always heading out to the woods. A lot of people thought it was unnatural for me to return to the scene of the accident, but it was like a touch stone, centering my world and helping me remember the last moments when I had felt happy, safe, and normal. I'd just been a girl, driving to her vacation cabin with her parents, singing to the radio.

I desperately wanted to find the guy who saved me. The kids at school called him a monster because of the scars I described covering his body. My desire to find him had landed me the moniker Monster Girl. At first, it hurt my feelings. He wasn't a monster, anyways. A monster wouldn't save someone's life. But as I got older, I chose to adopt the title. If I owned it, no one could use it to make fun of me anymore. Instead, they'd make fun of my streaked hair, piercings, or unusual makeup. In some places, my eclectic style might have made me cool, but here, in the Blue Ridge Mountains of Georgia, it made me weird and "alternative." But it kept me from self-harming, so my therapist would always tell my foster families to just leave me be.

The sun was starting to set, but I had finally made it to the part of Devil's Pass that wasn't marked off my map. I glanced at my watch. I still had time. Grabbing the flashlight out of my backpack, I continued further up the trail, taking me deeper into the forest.

I came out to these woods a lot, much to the chagrin of Lincoln, who hated bugs, too much sun, physical exercise, or really anything that fed him too much clean oxygen outside his college mancave.

We had both grown up outcasts for different reasons. Lincoln was an asthmatic kid with Coke bottle glasses and a mom who practically wrapped him in bubble wrap. His obsessively attentive mother wasn't really a big deal to me, a foster kid. At least someone gave a crap about him and what he was doing. Mrs. G was nice, although a little overprotective of her only child. And she always kept the pantry stocked with my favorite treats, gave me money to go to the movies with Lincoln, and bought my homecoming dress when my foster family at that time refused.

A crack of lightening split the sky, causing me to jump as the thunder roared behind it. The storm wasn't supposed to strike till later. A raindrop hit my cheek, then another. Pretty soon it was a torrential downpour. I pulled a poncho out of my pack and slipped my phone into the backpack for safekeeping. GPS wouldn't be any help to me if my phone shut off from being waterboarded.

It was hard to see, my flashlight's beam bouncing off the water droplets in front of me and unable to pierce the growing fog.

Lincoln's *I told you so* was already annoying me and he wasn't even around to say it. Which was a good thing, because he'd probably be freaking out at this point and puffing on his inhaler.

I carefully tried to pick my way along the trail, knowing it would be a long way back to my car. Assuming I could even find my way back down in all of this. It might be simpler to find a shelter and wait out the storm. I pulled my hoodie closer to my body, the wet fabric offering little shelter, despite the poncho.

In the distance, I thought I saw a weak glow. Shutting off my flashlight, I could see it more clearly. There was something in the distance, like a light from a cabin or something. I didn't realize there were any vacation spots up this far, but maybe I was in luck!

~~~~~

Nights like this reminded me of when I was brought to life over two centuries ago, and it wasn't a pleasant memory.

I loaded up the fireplace with more wood before setting the kettle on to boil. Storms put me on edge, and a nice cup of tea and an evening with the words of Lord Byron would be just the solution to help soothe my
~~~~~

rumpled spirits.

A banging on the door interrupted my plans. My body stiffened. No one should be out there, especially not on a night like this. In the twenty years since I had built this cabin, I had never once had a visitor. Perhaps if I ignored the knock, it would go away. After all, I had chosen this very spot because the trail to reach it was for experienced hikers only, and my—

"Hello, is anyone home?"

The knocking wasn't going away, it was just getting louder.

"Anyone home? I got caught in the storm and it's not really safe to find my way back to my car right now," the voice shouted over the storm. "I was hoping I could shelter here for a bit? Just until the storm clears up."

Ignoring the voice wasn't helping.

With a growl, I put a hoodie on, my hair falling in front of half my face, and pulled the hood up.

"Hello? Is anybody—"

I yanked the door open, and a sopping wet girl leaning with her ear to the wood stumbled in.

"Oh, hi," she said, trying to regain her footing.

"Are you going to come in? You're blocking the doorway and getting my floor wet with the rain."

Her eyebrows pulled together at the sound of my voice, and she cocked her head slightly.

Weirdo.

"I-I'm… sorry?" she stuttered.

"My floor," I pointed to the puddle beneath her muddied shoes. "You're getting it wet."

As if my words finally penetrated whatever fog was in her brain, the girl sprang into action, sidestepping the door so I could close it.

"I'm so sorry, sir. Do you have a towel? I can clean it up. I'm so sorry, I just—"

"Sit down." I cut her off, placing a towel on the barstool for her to sit.

"Thanks," she said, taking her wet poncho off. "Where should I put my backpack and—"

"Just set it down by the door."

"Okay, thanks," she replied, her brows still doing a weird dance every time I spoke.

What was her problem, anyway?

The kettle started squealing, reminding me of my ruined plans for the evening. I hated people. I especially hated having someone in my home.

"Man, your house is really hidden up here. I've been up this trail a couple times and never seen it."

I mostly ignored the words coming out of her mouth. It was easy enough to do while I prepared my tea.

Should I make her a cup too? I didn't really feel like it. She wasn't a guest. She was an invader. But I was also not a rude person. I waffled back and forth in my mind, her rambling white noise distracting from my predicament. Maybe if I gave her a cup of tea she would at least shut up for a few minutes?

I prepared a second cup and then stretched out my hand, offering the warm beverage.

The girl stopped talking, looking at the cup, surprised.

"Do you not like tea?" That was the problem with kids nowadays. They just wanted all of that fizzy crap. No appreciation for culture.

"I do, actually," she replied. As she reached out for the teacup and saucer, her eyes locked on the thin white scars slashed across the top of my hand and up the exposed portion of my arms.

I hated when people stared. "Do you want it?" I growled, startling her.

She quickly took the offering, and I pulled my sleeve down over my hand, covering my scars.

Not to be rude, but she wasn't exactly the most normal-looking person I'd ever met in my life, either. Her makeup was dark — edgy, some would say? She had tattoos across her wrists, and her ripped-up black jeans looked like someone had puked up various zippers, chains, straps, and buckles all over them. And then there was her hoodie —

Her hoodie… It was draped over her like a well-worn blanket, and it was identical to my own. Like, not just the same brand, but *identical* to the one I was wearing. Right size. Right color. Just more worn. Aged.

I could hear the wails like they were yesterday, and recalled the look of terror in those doe brown eyes. She was different now. Older. Her blond curls were now streaked with pinks and purples, and a hoop pierced through her nose, but her eyes were the same… and they recognized me.

She got off the stool, kicking off her shoes and carrying her teacup with her to warm up by the fire, surveying the floor-to-ceiling shelves of books in my living room. "You like books, huh?"

Her question was so natural, so unphased, it threw me. What was this girl doing here? How had she found me? *Why* had she found me?

I needed to stay calm.

"Some of these are in other languages, too," she continued, oblivious to the tailspin she had put me in. "Do you know more than one language?"

Who was this girl, and how was she so calm? Humans either ran the other way in fear when they saw me, or they recoiled. She was doing neither. She was… comfortable?

I didn't know what else to do, so I answered her. "Yes. I taught myself to read, and eventually learned other languages. It helps pass the time."

"That's pretty cool," she replied, and sipped her tea with her pinky finger extended. It was a conflicting image to see her punky persona sipping tea from my pastel green teacup with the fluted edges and soft bumblebee pattern. She pulled my/her hoodie closer around her body, as if it were a comfort blanket. "I'm Kat, by the way."

I knew the social nicety was to give her my name back, but I didn't feel like it. "I don't like cats."

"What?" she cried, startling me as her volume and energy rose suddenly and my delicate teacup clattered loudly against its matching saucer. "How can you not like cats? Have you ever had one?"

Her passion on the subject was jarring, but I was more worried about my teacup.

"N-no."

"Then you don't *know* that you don't like cats, do you?" she replied, plopping down on my living room floor with her legs crisscrossed, warming her back by the fire.

"I suppose not." What sort of sorcery was this? Somehow, despite me not wanting to talk to this girl, she was drawing a conversation out of me with ease. "Could you please be careful with that teacup?"

The girl glanced down at the cup and saucer in her hands. "Oh, sure. Is it special or something?"

"It matches the rest of my tea set and is impossible to replace."

"What, they don't make them anymore or something?"

"They do not," I replied, trying to ease some of the tension from my body.

"Cool. I'll be careful. So, what's your story?"

The ease with which she could alter a conversation was impressive.

I shrugged, finishing up my tea and pouring another from the kettle. "No story."

"Oh, come on," she persisted. "Everyone has a story. For example. Me, I'm a foster kid. I've worked my way through college— technical engineering if you're interested— and work part time at the Bob's Diner in town as a server. Job's not great, and neither is the food, honestly, but the tips are nice. Have you ever eaten there?"

How could this girl ramble so much? "No. I don't get out much."

"That's too bad. Not about the not eating there part, but the not getting out much. You should. Anyways, I grew up passed around from foster family to foster family after my parents died. Guess I didn't adjust well. My best friend Lincoln kinda helped me get through life—he's a total nerd, but he's a loyal one—and now I spend my time hiking these mountains looking for…" She trailed off for a moment, her eyes focusing on me as she rubbed the sleeve hem of her hoodie between her fingers. It seemed habitual, by the absentminded way she did it, as well as the distinct wear spot on the hem of the garment, as if she had spent years using that exact coping mechanism.

The girl switched thoughts, jarring me with her abrupt change in conversation. "And I have a cat who sleeps with me every night. Your turn."

"I'm not that interesting," I replied, somewhat amused by the girl's refreshingly forward personality. She was unlike most humans I had met, and oddly, I felt a sense of responsibility for the girl. Perhaps because of our shared past, something I didn't have with most people.

"Oh, I don't believe that. You look like you have some stories to tell, Mr…?" Her voice was serious, and her lingering question persistent.

"I go by Adam."

"Adam. Cool. Like I said, my name is Kat. I also go by Monster Girl."

I stiffened. "Monster Girl?"

She shrugged. "Yeah, growing up, kids called me that. I used to tell stories about a guy with scars all over his body, who saved me. He had dual-colored eyes and was bigger and stronger than anyone I had ever met before. I wanted to find him. It kinda became my life's mission. Everyone told me I was crazy, and the kids started saying I believed in Bigfoot. So, Monster Girl stuck."

People were cruel. Even to their own kind. Her story moved me as I remembered a time when humanity had treated me similarly, ridiculing my differences. Rejecting me. And yet, despite her hardships, there was still a goodness about this girl, like life hadn't hardened her soul yet.

"Do you have dual-colored eyes?" she asked.

There was no sense hiding it. The girl already knew who I was. I pulled the hood off my head, brushing back the long hair hiding half my face to reveal the jagged scar running at an angle across my features, and the two different colored eyes that had once belong to two different men.

"I'm sorry they were cruel to you."

Her expression was unafraid as she looked at me without horror or disgust. "And I'm sorry for whatever made you feel like you need to hide away from the world." Her voice was soft. Tender.

For the first time since I could remember, I felt a kinship to a human. The loneliness I carried through life felt especially heavy in that moment.

"What happened to you?" she whispered.

She made me want to confide in her. To lighten my load, if only for a moment, and unburden myself of my story. "You wouldn't believe it if I told you."

"Try me, I've seen some things."

People already believed the girl was crazy. If I shared my story and she told someone, they would probably just laugh it off as another crazy story. And if she caused too much trouble, I could just pick up and leave, like I had so many times before, despite becoming quite cozy in my remote little cabin over the years. It was a risk, but the burden of my story felt so heavy in that moment. I wanted to share it with someone. It had been so long since anyone had heard it.

I glanced at the bookshelves. "Have you ever read *Frankenstein*?"

"By Mary Shelley? Yeah, who hasn't? It's like required reading in school."

Great. Who wouldn't want an inaccurate version of their story told to school children? "Well, sometimes stories like that are based in reality." I took another sip of my tea.

"Sure. There's lots of children's books like that. Not that *Frankenstein* is exactly a kid's book."

No. It wasn't. "What if I told you *Frankenstein* wasn't a made-up story, but rather a family history passed down to the granddaughter of Dr. William Godwin? The names of her family were, of course, changed, and several embellishments were made for dramatic effect, but *Frankenstein* is actually the fantasied version of my origin story."

I wasn't sure what I expected. Perhaps for Kat to laugh at me, or run screaming, knowing how this wretched body of mine was created, but neither of those things occurred.

"So you're saying you're Frankenstein?"

"You know Frankenstein is not the name of the monster, right? Frankenstein, or rather Godwin, was the name of the scientist who created the monster out of dead parts of other people and reanimated them. He never gave him— me— a name."

"Yeah, I always thought that really sucked for him. Seemed kind of dehumanizing."

"I think it was easier for the doctor not to see me as alive. I repulsed him."

"Yeah, well, you seem pretty alive to me. So why Adam?"

This girl never seemed to run out of questions. "I asked my creator to impart to me a name, for I was like his Adam."

"Adam from like the Bible?"

"Yes, from the Genesis origin story. But my creator refused. Over the years, I just adopted that name. Seemed fitting, somehow."

"So you're, like, super old, then. That's why you know so many languages. You've had a lot of time on your hands."

"Yes, unfortunately. It seems I am ageless."

"And that's why you live all the way up here by yourself?"

"No… I got tired of no one being able to look at me without horror. It's just easier to live life as a recluse when there is no changing these." I pointed to the scars on my body.

"And yet you stopped to help me, the night my parents died…

Why?" There were tears in her eyes.

"Because I just couldn't sit back and hear your pain without doing something about it... I could hear my own pain in your cries."

Silence hung heavy for a moment between us. All was quiet.

"Well." Kat broke the silence, getting up from her seated position on the floor. "The storm has stopped, and my clothes, thanks to your fire, are dry. I probably should be heading home."

In the glow of Kat's conversational skills, I hadn't even noticed that the storm had passed. I felt a heaviness in my chest, seeing her grab her backpack to leave.

I followed her toward the door. "Are you sure you can find your way to your car in the dark?"

"Oh yeah. I always drop a pin on my phone's GPS. Won't be a problem at all."

"Well, be safe, then," I offered, unsure what else to say or how to process the emotions inside me. "I don't want to have to save you a third time."

Kat smiled, then startled me by throwing her arms around my waist and pulling me close in an embrace. "Thank you, Adam. You have no idea how much tonight meant to me."

The sensation of human contact overloaded my senses. The last time I had held someone was the night I pulled her frightened form from the wreckage of the car accident.

"And I promise to keep your secret," she whispered against the fabric of my hoodie.

When she let go of me, my world felt cold and empty again.

"And just so you know," she added, opening the cabin door and pausing for a moment. "Someone who saves people isn't a monster."

And just like that, Kat was gone, her shoes squeaking with every step she took down the trail to her own life.

Someone who saves people isn't a monster... Her words rolled around in my head the rest of the night and into the morning as I struggled with an existential crisis. I had always been the monster. I had seen myself as the monster more than I ever saw myself as Adam. Maybe because it was easier to accept my creator's disdain for me if I was unlovable, rather than just being discarded as trash. A disappointment.

No one had really loved me. Certainly no one had spent their life searching for me. The night I left my creator was a relief for him. And yet, all these years later, it seemed my soul had been tied to another and I never even knew.

I reflected on the way she used my hoodie to comfort herself, often rubbing in the same worn spot on the sleeve hem. Or how she would pull the sleeves around her small frame like a pair of arms hugging her. That plain old black hoodie had received more love over the years than I had in my entire existence, bringing new meaning to the phrase, 'beauty is in the eye of the beholder.'

Eventually, I drifted off to sleep as the sun was rising, my entire routine thrown off by the hurricane of a girl who had turned everything about me upside-down. But once again, my plans seemed not my own for the first time in decades.

A knocking at my door startled me awake.

Now who was at my door? This better not become a habit or I for sure would have to relocate—

Kat stood at the door, a large white ball of fluff cradled in her arms. She looked even more unusual in the daylight with her multi-colored hair pulled up into a ponytail, revealing metal studs lining her ears and thick black liner rimming her dark eyelashes.

"So, I decided you need a pet. I'm totally not okay with you being up here alone all the time."

Without invitation, Kat entered my cabin, dropping her hiking pack on the floor. I was so elated to see her — a new and interesting emotion for me—that I just stood there, listening to her ramble.

"And since I'm such a fan of cats, and you're undecided, I thought maybe I should bring Fat Louie with me to try to convert you. His name's Fat Louie, after the cat in *The Princess Diaries*. Have you ever seen it? If not, we're going to have to watch it. It's Louie's favorite. You have a TV out here, right?" Kat stopped long enough to breathe, her grumpy looking cat still in her arms. "Were you sleeping?"

I closed the door behind her. "Would you and Fat Louie like some tea?"

The End

FRANKENSTEIN'S MANOR
Jim Doran

The Halloween attraction my friends and I visited in the suburbs of Michigan wasn't truly haunted, but it was far from normal.

The ritual of frequenting several haunted houses was a time-honored event among my friends during October. We had started this tradition while attending community college and continued it during our professional careers. The five of us selected a weekend night and chose the scariest attractions in the area. This year was different in two ways.

The first was a chance encounter inside a Halloween store during September. When I reached for the perfect cape to complete my Phantom of the Opera costume, another patron went to pick up the same item. Only one hung on the display, and the other shopper, a young woman, apologized. I hadn't noticed her before, but when we both explained why we thought the cape completed our ensemble, I recognized a fellow horror aficionado—one with a stunning pair of doe-brown eyes behind thick glasses.

We needed the cape on different nights, so we struck a deal to purchase it together and trade it off. After exchanging phone numbers, we texted each other about our respective Halloween parties. A request for a first date followed.

My new girlfriend, May, fit right into my gaggle of goofball friends, and she loved the idea of traveling to several attractions in a single night. As I said, her presence was the first difference from most years as "Thad" became "Thad and May." The second difference was far more bizarre.

I don't know if Eliza, part of my circle of friends, resented our dating or was oblivious to how it changed the dynamic. But when the time came to part ways for the night, she suggested one more attraction. May and I were hoping for a few hours alone, but Eliza persisted, and our other friends' subtle clues did nothing to influence her. May relented and found a site named Frankenstein's Manor, five miles from what was to be our last gathering of the season. Everyone besides May, Eliza, and I said they were going to retire for the night and we said our goodbyes.

Similar to most haunted houses, Frankenstein's Manor was in a repurposed building. In this case, the location was an old, abandoned library. This setting made the "manor" seem more targeted to middle graders and less gruesome than the rest we frequented that night.

Nonetheless, we exited the car.

Eliza snorted. "This looks stupid. Let's go somewhere else."

May caught my eye, and I immediately squelched the idea. "We either enter this place or call it a night, Eliza."

She tucked in her T-shirt with a depiction of a three-dimensional knife embedded in her chest. "You're no fun anymore, Thad. I remember when you used to like *real* haunted houses."

I shuffled, and May broke the tension with a suggestion. "Let's take a selfie with the building in the background."

Eliza, May, and I squished together, and May took the picture. My girlfriend and I were all smiles, my arm around her frame, but Eliza ruined the picture with a curled upper lip.

May examined the photograph. "Maybe we should take another, and all smile this time?"

"I *was* smiling," snapped Eliza. "Taking pictures at a haunted house is for high schoolers. We're more serious about our outings than most."

I should've warned May. Eliza was opinionated to the point of being insufferable. My friends and I had grown up with it, and her critical comments rolled off our backs. But from the lines around May's mouth, I could tell she was taking a lot of her comments personally.

"Take it easy, Eliza," I remarked. "May likes taking pictures, and I'm glad she does."

Eliza shrugged.

We entered the short queue and were soon at the point of entry where the employees were taking payment. A man dressed in scrubs told us the cost of entry and swiped my card on his phone. His medical halogen light affixed to his head served the dual purpose of costume and illumination.

While I signed the screen on the phone, Eliza asked, "This isn't a stupid attraction for little kids, is it? I mean, who uses Frankenstein these days to scare people? Frankenstein is so old-fashioned."

The doctor shone his light into our eyes when he looked up. "You don't have to go inside if you're frightened."

Eliza leaned on the table and raised her voice. "I survived all five levels of The Bloody Asylum, including the snake level and the rope bridge to the exit. You're mistaken if you think some teenager wearing a Frankenstein mask will freak me out. I've come out of Terror Park and Gruesome Grove laughing."

The doctor shrugged and took his phone from me. "Your funeral."

Eliza tossed her straight golden hair dismissively over her shoulder.

"Let's keep an open mind," said May.

Eliza pointed at the remodeled library. "This place costs as much as the others we've been to tonight. If it sucks, I'm reviewing it on Yelp before we get to the car."

From the expression on the doctor's face, I was afraid he was going to refund our money and ask us to leave. I took Eliza's elbow and led her to the entrance. "Come on."

As we waited at the door, I caught Eliza's eye. "Why do you have to be like that?"

"Like what?"

"Can't you enjoy being here no matter how scary it is?"

Eliza put a hand on her hip. "Dude, Frankenstein isn't frightening in the least. Those old movies with a lumbering idiot with his eyes half-closed? Come on. Not a drop of blood anywhere. How is that terrifying?"

May bit her lip. "You should have more respect. Those movies had solid writing and fantastic sets. They're a lot better than you remember."

Eliza put her hands out and swayed back and forth as if sleepwalking. "I'm after the dimwitted girl, but I move as fast as a snail." She dropped her hands. "Can you just feel the tension in the air?"

"Chill, Eliza." I crossed my arms. "Frankenstein's monster happens to be one of my favorites. By the way, you're describing the creature. The *doctor*'s name is Frankenstein."

Eliza rolled her eyes. "I stand corrected. News flash. Who cares?"

We paused before the entrance while a breeze brushed past us. May rummaged in her purse while Eliza popped a piece of bubblegum in her mouth. The door opened, and a gangly teen used a flashlight to direct the three of us inside. Without another word, we entered a dark hallway. The entrance shut, extinguishing all ambient light. I led with May's hands on my shoulders and Eliza next to her. I waited for my eyes to adjust before moving forward.

"Yawn," said Eliza. She raised her voice. "As if I haven't been in a dark hallway a million times tonight."

We advanced down the corridor until a bright light illuminated a scene to our right. A small room held an oblong operating table with a mannequin standing next to it. Waxy and wearing a bad toupee, the figure held a needle. On the table lay a mammoth shape of a man covered with a white sheet. Electricity noises buzzed to life.

A man's high-pitched voice interrupted the soundtrack. "They called me crazy. Crazy, am I? I will give life to my creation."

The lighting dimmed, and the soundtrack faded. Eliza groaned. "Are you kidding me? This is scary? This wouldn't frighten Scooby-Doo."

While her statement was accurate, I wasn't going to give her the satisfaction of agreeing. "Come on, Eliza. We're here to have fun. Go with it."

She pointed at the display—its lights fading. "They can't even afford to hire live actors. We paid the same admission as other places with real people. At least they move."

The diorama descended into darkness. Another light came on ahead of us, and I spotted a neon green arrow and moved in the direction it pointed. May ran her hand along my arm and grabbed my fingers.

Eliza huffed behind me. "This is how we end our night?"

I reached a bend in the enclosed hallway and rounded the corner with the rest on my heels. To my left, a metal door with spray-painted words "do not enter" barred any further progress. I reasoned it must be an exit.

I shuffled past, but Eliza's hand landed on my shoulder. "We should go through that door."

A rule-follower, May snapped, "Absolutely not. We came here to see the attraction, not get thrown out."

"The so-called attraction is lame." Eliza popped a bubble from her gum with a crack as if adding an audible exclamation point to her opinion.

My goal was to proceed through the exhibit, return to my car, and salvage a little private time with May. "Let's go, Eliza."

Undeterred, she turned, opened the door, and rushed through. Stark white light filled the passage beyond.

May shook her head, and though we hadn't known each other for very long, I could almost read her thoughts. *She's your friend. You talk some sense into her.*

I sighed, sidled past May, and entered the well-lit corridor. To my surprise, she kept hold of my hand and followed me inside. Eliza walked ahead, her arms extended and fingers running across the featureless walls. Ceiling lights, inset into the corkboard above, shone down on her. No graffiti on the walls, no dry ice tricks, no darkness. The hallway was as sterile as a hospital.

The door clicked shut after May entered, and I followed Eliza. "Eliza, we're not supposed to be here, and this place is boring anyway."

She glanced over her shoulder and winked at me. "I'm hoping this leads behind the scenes. We'll scare some of the employees. Serves them right for constructing a junior haunted house and naming it after a wimpy monster."

"Eliza…"

But she wasn't listening to me. When she had an idea, Eliza was like a submarine missile aimed at its target. Come hell or high water, she planned on pranking someone. I only hoped we wouldn't find anyone back here, so we could return to the attraction's central passageway.

Our route turned right, and Eliza led the way while smacking her gum. A similarly lit corridor with a low-hanging tiled ceiling led thirty feet down to another bend. I wasn't sure where we were inside the library anymore.

"Hey, look!" Eliza held out the hem of her shirt. The illustration of the knife had vanished, leaving nothing in its place. "Weird. Where'd the graphic go? Must be the lighting. And I don't remember this shirt coming down to the middle of my thighs."

While forming a response, I spied a man amble around the corner at the end. Dressed up as Frankenstein's monster, the man wore a black, bulky jacket, torn pants, and large boots. Thinning black hair draped down his square-shaped head, framing sunken cheeks and dark-encircled eyes. The rounded bolts on the sides of his neck topped off the ensemble. All in all, the costume and makeup were excellent.

We halted, and he mimicked our actions, his lip snarling. Full of bravado when she had entered, Eliza now stood still. I shouldered my way past her, forming an excuse to keep us from being ejected.

"Uh, sorry. We're lost. Is this the right way?"

The man didn't respond but clenched his fists. He marched forward, not with his arms raised in a sleepwalker stance but like a man on a mission. The wrath in his eyes unnerved me, and I wondered if he might not understand English.

"Run!" breathed May.

We all spun around to flee, but the man grabbed my collar and pulled me back. I was shocked. I thought employees had a no-touch rule. Manhandling a patron was a serious offense in a haunted attraction.

I shook him off and turned around. "We were just leaving."

The man ignored me and put his hands around my neck. I grabbed his wrists. "Hey, buddy! Knock it—"

But I couldn't speak another word. His fingers clamped down on my windpipe in an iron grip, and I trembled, realizing he was strong enough to snap my neck. He applied pressure to block my airway. I put my hands on his face, at least a foot above me, and pushed, but I might as well have been shoving a mountain. He didn't budge.

No air to call for help. This was the end. A crazed employee was about to strangle me to death. I forgot about May or Eliza, focusing on my survival. I couldn't move this golem of a man, and I slapped his face with my palm.

Hiss. An acrid-scented breeze of something blew past me at the strangler. He roared, releasing me. I fell to the ground and caught my breath.

"Don't look up," warned May. "Pepper spray."

I swallowed lungsful of air while the employee stumbled backward, screaming.

Grabbing my hand, May pulled me away from the spray. "We have to get out of here."

Eliza paused at the bend, and we raced toward her. We needed to escape this madhouse and call the police. Forget the no-touch policy. This guy hadn't even negotiated or warned me. He had said nothing at all, charging at me.

When we rounded the corner, we expected to see the door back to the main hallway. Instead, the corridor terminated in a T-intersection. Where the door had been was now a blank wall.

The three of us approached the intersection in a mad scramble. May slapped her hands against the drywall, screaming for help. When she caught her breath, she asked, "Where's the door?"

Behind us, footsteps scraped across the corridor we had just vacated.

Reaching over May, I ran my fingers along the barrier, searching for a seam. "I don't know."

Eliza peered both ways down the intersecting corridor. "There must be another exit. Let's go right and put some distance between this psycho and us."

We ran in the direction she had indicated, and the path turned right again. Footsteps echoed behind us, not rushing, but steady on the stone floor. We continued forward, hoping the crazed employee would stop following us. We made our way left, then right. The footfalls of the man chasing us beat out a steady rhythm.

And then the footsteps stopped. The three of us halted, and I cocked my head to listen closely. I put a finger to my lips. Perhaps we could sneak out without our pursuer knowing.

We waited, holding our breaths as long as possible. May hugged her arms, and Eliza bunched up a handful of her T-shirt, now extending down past her knees. I tried each of our phones. No signal.

Handing the phones back, I concentrated on listening. At some point, I reasoned, I would hear the madman's footsteps and that would decide our next move. Waiting was the perfect plan until someone smashed his fist through the wall near May.

We all yelled while splintered wood flew everywhere, and the bleached hand with black fingernails clawed at us, snagging a fistful of May's hair. She released a high-pitched scream while her head was yanked forcefully toward the hole.

Through the opening, the features of the disturbed employee glared at us. At this point, I didn't care whether he was a person or a monster. I only knew we had to escape.

With a forceful pull, May ripped herself free, leaving the clenched fist with a handful of her hair.

None of us needed to say a word as we raced away. We rushed down passageways, turning corner after corner and taking turns calling for help. Each corridor seemed narrower than the one before. Would they ever end? We kept together, and Eliza stumbled once with fatigue. I feared we'd never find an exit.

In the hallways we vacated, the thudding of heavy boots never faded. No matter how fast we sprinted, the man remained behind us, just around the last corner.

Eventually, we came to a long hallway terminating at a solid oak door. As we reached it, the figure chasing us came into view and growled.

I hurried the women inside, hardly taking in the square room with white walls and fluorescent lighting. Slamming the door after us, I spied a deadbolt. I turned it moments before the figure on the other side smashed into the oak panel. The latching mechanism held but shook in its plating. It wouldn't hold for long.

Swinging around, I noticed a weird contraption in the center of this refuge of drywall and modern-theater starkness. Two five-foot-tall silver bars extended from the floor, each topped with a large sphere. The hum of electricity buzzed through the metal. In graffiti on the far wall, someone had scrawled a message:

To return to where you were, complete the circuit.

May turned pale. "No."

The madman pounded on the other side of the door, and the entire barrier trembled, with flakes of wood falling to the ground. May jumped, and I swore and stepped away.

Eliza stiffened. "We're trapped."

I ran my hand along a smooth wall. "There must be some other way out."

May also began searching, but Eliza didn't join us. Instead, she eyed the metal bars. "I don't think we're going to find another way."

Moving along the walls, I knocked, hoping for a hollow sound. "Eliza, electricity is running through the bars. Who knows how much?"

But I stopped when she approached the globes.

Eliza's eyes glazed over as she stepped forward. She avoided stepping on the fringe of her T-shirt, now centimeters above the floor. She reached for the metal rods.

"But electricity brings power. I want…power."

"Eliza!"

She touched one of the spheres and extended her hand to the other globe. I stepped forward to stop her, but our pursuer hit the door again, and this time the deadbolt snapped.

A terror-filled moan escaped my lips as the door sprang open to reveal Frankenstein's creation. I froze in place, eyeing the monster as it drew closer.

However, Eliza didn't pause, placing her hand on the other sphere.

The electricity coursed through her and she convulsed. Her gum popped from her mouth and hit the floor as her hair frizzed and stood up. Her body shook violently, eyes rolling back in her head, and with a spark and a smell of ozone, she dropped to the floor.

The ceiling lights dimmed when she fell, and the hulking creature rushed to her, ignoring May and me. Eliza, her shirt now a long gown resembling a sheet, slumped on the ground. Electricity had fried her hair until it stood upright and singed her lips black.

The monstrous man grunted, hovering over our friend. With one swift move, he leaned down and scooped her up. I should've fought for her, but with the tender way he held Eliza, I was too stunned to do anything but watch.

The Frankenstein monster eyed us, his expression making it clear that Eliza was now his. His attention shifted to a blank wall to our left. From the corner of my eye, I spotted an exit that hadn't existed before. After everything that had happened since we veered off the path, I didn't question it.

Turning, the Frankenstein monster carried Eliza away, retreating down the corridor where we had entered. He moved to the end of the hallway, rounded a corner, and then silence replaced his steady footsteps.

The tips of May's fingers were in her mouth. "What…just happened?"

I squeezed her other hand. "I don't know." With some effort, I pushed aside the questions I couldn't answer. "We're going to get the police. We'll report it."

When May and I exited, we found ourselves in the main attraction with its slipshod walls and poor lighting. We had passed through the same door we had gone through when trespassing.

We reversed our steps, past the diorama of the mannequin and pushed past people trying to enter.

Ignoring their protests, I slammed my fist on the table where the doctor-costumed employee sat. "Call the police!"

People stepped away and gave us room, murmuring and whispering.

The doctor reared back. "Hey, take it easy."

May stood next to me, glaring, and I pointed at the library. "One of your costumed freaks kidnapped my friend. If you don't call the police, I will."

The doctor lowered his eyebrows and then looked at May. "Your friend's right there."

I swore. "No. The other woman who was with us."

"What other woman?"

May produced her cell phone and held it toward the doctor to allow him to view the selfie we had taken earlier. "Her!"

The doctor examined the photograph and then shifted his attention to May. "It's you."

"What?" May flipped her cell phone around. In the picture, only May and I stood together smiling. No one occupied the space where Eliza once stood, but on the ground was a woman's shadow, wrapped in a long, draping sheet.

The End

FIX AND REFRESH
Pam Halter

2:00am Friday, October 18

Frank opened his eyes to see the sickle moon peeking through the blinds. That dream again! The one where he was standing in a field and there were people lined up to talk to him. He didn't know any of them, but they all seemed to know him.

He fluffed his pillow and tried to go back to sleep. Tomorrow was the grand opening of his bookstore. He needed to be alert and awake.

9:00am The Grand Opening

"Hi, welcome to Chapters and Pages!" Frank said for the hundredth time. The door jingled as person after person came in. Everyone chattered and talked about the bookstore. They were so happy to have one in their little town of Geneva.

"Mr. Steinbrook, can you help me find a book about pirate ships?" an eight-year-old boy asked. "Me and my grandpa used to read pirate books." He looked down for a moment. "Before he died."

"Sure!" Frank replied. "I bet you had some great times with your grandpa."

The boy told Frank his name was Timmy. Timmy Shoemaker. Frank had the strangest feeling of déjà vu. It grew stronger as he pulled out an age-appropriate book and handed it to Timmy.

The day went on, and often he had the feeling he'd had similar conversations with people—strangers—or he'd helped them find a book that was familiar to him even though he'd never read it.

The freakiest part of the day was when he had given a middle-aged woman, Mrs. Ratherly, a cookbook for seafood. He had glanced at his hands and got the feeling they weren't his. For a couple of seconds, he couldn't feel his fingers. Then it passed. His hands were okay, but he didn't *feel* okay.

As he turned the key to lock up for the evening, he reflected over the day. It had been a great success. He knew it wouldn't be as busy every day as it had been today, but it was clear Geneva needed this bookstore.

As he pulled the key out of the lock, he had the same feeling about his hands.

"Stop it," he said out loud. "Stop it!"

He shoved the key into his pants pocket and began the short walk to the convenience store for a snack.

His loafers clicked on the sidewalk as he strode. He liked the sound. It was comfortable. Familiar.

But how could it be? These shoes were brand new. He'd never worn loafers before. He had thought he needed something a bit nicer for the store.

Frank slowed his steps. Again, the feeling as though part of his body wasn't his. First his hands, and now his feet. He stood on the edge of the circle of light from the streetlamp. Was he imagining things?

3:30am, Monday, October 21
Again. That dream.

Frank got a glass of water from the kitchen. He wiped his sweating forehead with a tea towel. What in the world was going on with his dreams? This time he dreamed he was reading the pirate book from the store to a young boy. Not Timmy, but a boy the same age with the same brown, curly hair and freckled nose. And in his dream, Frank *knew* the boy. Loved him.

Like a son.

Frank's hands shook as he pulled the sheet and blanket back over himself. It had been some years since he had prayed. Perhaps he needed to return to that habit.

4:00pm, Wednesday, December 16
"Yes, Storytime starts at 10am every Saturday," Frank answered the woman on the phone. "Yes, it's for ages preschool through eight or nine years. Hope to see you there!"

After two months, Chapters and Pages was still going strong. The introduction of Storytime was a success; every Saturday the children's room was almost full.

He wanted so much to call his father and brag, but it wouldn't be worth it. Papa never gave him encouragement or praise. Sometimes Frank felt like he wasn't even his son.

Frank loved reading to the children. He did different voices for all the characters, read with lots of emotion and energy. The parents seemed to enjoy it as well. Things were going smoothly, and he had had no more episodes of feeling like parts of his body weren't his, or feelings of déjà vu. In fact, he felt completely in control, which was a relief.

He had decorated the store for Christmas, chosen lots of Christmas books for Storytime, and even had plates of cookies on the counter from the local bakery down the street, Shirley's Sweeties. The owner, Shirley, was friendly and kind. She knew the names of all her customers, even the newbies.

She felt like a mother hen to Frank. Unlike the owners of the coffee shop, Drips, across the street. The Petersons. A married couple, in maybe their forties, they hardly ever gave him a smile or called a greeting.

And even though the store name was awful, the coffee was good and always hot, so Frank continued to go there for a cup in the morning.

The bell on the door jingled as *Jingle Bells* started playing over his sound system, which he found humorous. He grinned and called out, "Welcome to Chapters and Pages!" Still smiling, he looked up to see a young woman with dark brown, almost black, frizzy hair and large green eyes. She wore a multi-colored knitted shawl. His breath caught in his throat. He stared at her, unable to speak.

She smiled. "Hi, it's Frank, right? My mom, Shirley, you know, from Shirley's Sweeties, said this was a great bookstore. I'm excited there's one in town now."

Frank could only nod. His heartbeat felt strange, all fluttery and unrhythmic. It had never beat like that before.

"I'm Liz." She stuck out her hand, and her earrings tinkled. Tiny Christmas bells.

"Uh, um." Frank cleared his throat. "Yes. Frank. Thank you." As he grasped her hand, he felt a mild electric charge run up his arm. "Can I help you find anything?"

"Oh, that's so nice!" She flashed him another engaging smile. "I just wanted to stop in and say hello. I have errands to run, but I'll be back."

"Sure, sure," Frank stammered.

"Nice to meet you!" And with that, Liz was out the door before *Jingle Bells* had played the last chorus.

Frank shook his head. What had just happened?

9:00am, Thursday, December 17
Frank no sooner unlocked the door when *she* came in.

Liz.

Shirley's daughter. He had no idea Shirley had a husband, let alone a daughter.

"Morning, Frank!" Liz called out. "Does the offer of help still stand?"

The furnace hadn't warmed the store yet, but Frank felt flushed.

"Of course," he said. "I'll turn on the fireplace, then tell me what you're looking for."

"Oooooh, a fireplace! I love fireplaces!" Liz exclaimed. "Is it wood or gas?"

Frank clicked the switch and fire blazed forth. "I'm afraid it's gas." He turned and shrugged. "It's safer, though. Turns off immediately. I wouldn't want the building to catch fire."

After turning on the tree lights, he hung up his coat. "Now, what can

I help you find?"

Liz gazed at the angel on top of the tree. "Oh, I don't know. What's good?"

Frank opened his mouth and shut it. She gave a great rolling laugh. "I'm kidding! Where's the classic section? I'm in the mood for a good classic novel."

He directed her to the back wall, but he felt, well, weird. Something happened to him when she laughed. It had come from deep within her and rolled up her throat and out her mouth, making a sound of complete joy. It started a kind of buzzing in his brain. A nice buzzing.

The feeling continued through the morning. Liz was comfortably seated in one of the plush chairs and leafing through the pages of three novels: *Ben Hur, The Good Earth,* and *Wives and Daughters.* Frank wondered which one she would pick. He was pretty good at guessing what book a customer would buy, but he had no clue with Liz.

At noon, things got busy in the store, last minute Christmas shoppers rushing in on their lunchbreaks. Frank had decided to be closed from 7pm on December 24th to December 27th and reopen on the 28th.

At 2pm, he looked out the front window and noticed it had started snowing lightly. How nice. He hoped it would stick around for Christmas. He went to pick up his paper coffee cup, but it wasn't there. He looked up and Liz stood at the counter, smiling that dazzling smile, and holding two fresh steaming cups. Which, as the aroma hit him, were not coffee. Whipped cream topped each one, visible through the clear domes.

"Snow calls for hot chocolate!" Liz said. "Do you want peppermint or caramel?"

"Peppermint," he said. "My favorite. How did you know?"

She popped off the top of hers and took a sip, which left her with a thick white mustache. She licked it and giggled. "Lucky guess."

Frank's heart gave a lurch, and he grinned back. He wondered how long she would be in town. He felt drawn to her but wasn't ready to admit it yet.

That night, as he was brushing his teeth, he looked into the mirror and dropped his toothbrush. For half a second, he didn't recognize his reflection.

He spit water into the sink and looked at himself in the mirror again as he wiped his mouth. He didn't recognize his teeth! Then he was back to normal.

"I must be really tired," he said as he turned off the light.

6:00pm, Monday, December 21
The store was full, Christmas music played, the fireplace warmed the air, laughter and joy abounded. But Frank hadn't seen Liz all day. She had

come into the store every day since that first morning. Still hadn't made up her mind about which books she wanted. He had suggested *Little Women* or *Gone With the Wind*, but she had said she was still thinking. Then she would smile, and his heart would lurch, and it would have been perfectly fine if time had stopped right then and there.

He pulled out *A Christmas Carol* from a new shipment and set it aside as a gift for her. Somehow, he knew she would love it.

Five minutes before closing, the door jingled, and he knew it was her.

"Hey, Frank! Let's go get a late supper. It's about time we had a meal together."

No idea what she meant by that, but Frank decided to take the chance. Maybe he would find out when she was leaving. He had questioned Shirley about it, but she only said Liz was a free spirit.

As he slipped his arms into his coat, he shot up a quick prayer, as he had been doing more and more often, followed Liz out the door, then locked it.

The only place open for a meal was the Geneva Towne Diner several blocks away, so Liz called a cab and off they went.

"Let's do something fun," she said over her menu. "I'll order for you, and you order for me, but let's not tell each other. We can whisper it to our waitress."

"Sure," Frank said. And the feeling he was someone else came over him again as it had done frequently. Stronger since Liz came into his life.

Before Liz, Frank had lived a quiet life on a schedule, and quite predictable. Well, mostly predictable. Until he opened the bookstore and started feeling like his hands and feet weren't his. Or his thoughts were someone else's.

They small talked while they waited for their orders. When the food finally came, they both burst out laughing. They had ordered the exact same thing for each other: bacon cheeseburgers with onion rings and coleslaw.

"How did you know —" they said together.

"Frank," Liz said. "When we first met, did you feel like maybe you knew me?"

"What a strange question," he answered. "No, I don't think so. Why?"

Liz twirled an onion ring through ketchup. "Don't freak out, okay? But I feel a connection with you. It's never happened to me before. It's weird and okay at the same time."

"I don't feel connected to anyone," Frank lied. He wasn't going to say how he really felt about her. "Never have. I'm quite alone."

Liz's eyes opened wide. "Not even your parents?"

"I don't remember my mother." Frank folded his hands. He didn't want her to see how they trembled. "And my father was a — well — a serious man. I actually don't know him well."

The First Noel was playing on the diner sound system. Liz didn't say anything. Frank hoped he hadn't offended her, although he didn't know why she would be upset. He picked up his coffee cup.

"Gosh, Frank, I'm really sorry," Liz finally said. "I love my parents and they love me."

"What does your dad do?" The question was out before Frank could check himself. "If it's okay to ask." He nervously took a bite of his burger.

"Daddy used to work in a shoe factory," Liz said, quietly. "But he was killed in a car accident when I was eight years old."

It was Frank's turn to apologize. He wanted to take her hand and comfort her, but he would never presume.

His hand, however, **did** presume, and he almost gasped when he saw it holding hers. **His** hand would have not done such a thing. He snatched it back.

"What's wrong?" Liz's eyes searched his face.

Frank wiped his mouth with a napkin, his hands trembling violently. "It's — it's — I don't know. I can't say." He slid out of the booth. "I'm sorry, Liz. I can't stay. I don't know what's going on!"

He tossed a twenty on the table and darted out the door.

He ran all the way to his apartment over the bookstore.

He locked the door, rushed to his bedroom, and fell on his knees by the bed, folding the hands that were attached to his arms but didn't feel like his.

"Please, God, please help me!"

3:00pm, Tuesday, December 22nd

Another busy day at the store, but Liz hadn't come in at all. Frank thought he should feel relieved, but he didn't.

"Happy Christmas, Mr. Steinbrook!" called a customer as she went out the door.

Frank called back, "Happy Christmas!" without looking up, as he was busy wrapping a book for another customer. He enjoyed wrapping books. It was comforting, somehow. Funny that he couldn't remember where he had learned to do it.

He yawned. Too bad it was so close to Christmas, or he'd close early. He had the worst nightmare of all last night after he finally fell asleep. People were lined up to talk to him again, but this time they were demanding he give them back their hands, their feet, and other body parts. He kept trying to explain he didn't have them, but they all shouted at him. He had woken up in a sweat.

The door jingled and he called out a greeting, as usual. Then he froze.

He knew it was Liz before he looked up. He handed the wrapped book to the elderly woman, thanked her, and turned to his right.

"Hey," she said.

"Hey."

"I wanted to say see ya and wish you a Happy Christmas," she went on.

See ya?

Frank swallowed. "Aren't you staying for Christmas?"

She shrugged. "I was going to ... but now ..."

There was no one at the counter, so Frank came out from behind it. "I'm sorry for my outburst last night. It really had nothing to do with you."

She smiled. "I didn't think it had."

"So, why aren't you staying?"

She ran a finger along the edge of the wooden counter. "I don't know if you'd understand."

Frank's heart leaped up in his chest. In that second, he felt a definite connection with her. He knew he only had seconds to keep this woman from leaving his life forever. Somehow, he knew it.

Did he want that? She had only been around for a week. But it felt longer. Did he want to lose that? If he let her go, his life could go back to being peaceful and in order.

And alone.

And ordinary.

No!

He cleared his throat. "Would you wait? I'd like to take you to dinner again tonight. And I promise no outbursts, okay?"

Now she really smiled. "Okay."

After they ordered, Frank took a sip of water. His treacherous, unfamiliar hands were numb. Liz might think him crazy, but he had to tell someone. He had to tell her.

"I want to share something with you," he said. "And hear me out before you say anything, okay?"

Liz blotted her lips with a napkin. "Sounds intriguing!"

Frank smiled. "Don't laugh at me."

She just sat there, waiting. Well, okay then. He told her what was happening to him. How he felt as if parts of his body were unfamiliar. How total strangers *were* familiar. His nightmares. His sketchy memory of his youth.

"I'm only thirty-five years old," he said. "I can't be going senile already, can I?"

The waiter brought them two root beers. Liz ran her finger around the rim of her mug. Frank took a breath. But before he could say anything, she spoke.

"I believe you."

That took Frank back. "What? Really?"

"I have something to share with you now," she continued. "I'm not really Shirley's daughter. Not biologically. I'm adopted. She adopted me when I was fifteen."

That surprised Frank, but he didn't show it.

The waiter came with their salads.

Liz reached for the salt. "I couldn't have asked for a better mom."

Frank nodded.

"But something's pulled at me for years. Since I got adopted. A feeling that something's missing. That I'm not whole." She tapped her fork on the table. "And those memories of my dad? I don't think they're mine."

Now Frank couldn't hide his surprise. "What makes you think that?"

"Because Shirley has never been married."

That threw Frank for a loop. "Never? I can't believe it."

Liz shrugged. "Yeah, well, maybe she just never met the right guy."

They sat in silence for a few moments. Then Liz said, "Shirley got me out of foster care. I guess I dreamed about having a dad."

"My dreams have been disturbing lately." Frank stabbed a piece of tomato. "And what you said about not feeling whole? Yeah. That's what I couldn't put into words."

She smiled faintly.

"So ..." He hesitated a moment. "Sorry if this is too personal, but how old are you now?" He chuckled. "I'm not good at guessing peoples' ages."

"It's okay. I was thirty in September."

A large crowd of people came into the restaurant, laughing and singing *Joy to the World*. Frank buttered a piece of crusty bread. He waited for Liz to go on, but she was concentrating on eating her salad.

He pondered her words for a moment more. "So, what do we do?"

She looked up from her bowl. "I don't know. I'm not even sure why I came home. Just felt drawn."

Frank smiled. "I felt drawn to Shirley the first time I met her in the bakery. She feels, well, comfortable."

The waiter brought their entrees.

"Mmmmm ... I love spaghetti," they said together, then laughed.

Over their meal, they talked about their childhood Christmas customs. They both opened one gift on Christmas Eve. They both loved Christmas pancakes, which consisted of buttermilk pancakes topped with green icing and dotted with maraschino cherries.

"Now that's weird," Frank said. "I mean, lots of people open gifts on Christmas Eve. But the pancakes? It almost feels ... creepy."

"It really does," Liz agreed. "I haven't had those nasty, syrupy sweet pancakes for years. Why did I love them?"

Frank cracked up. "No idea. We do weird things when we're kids."

Their waitress brought them cups of decaf and two slices of tiramisu.

"This is way better than pancakes," Liz said. And they both laughed again.

As Frank sipped his decaf, he remembered the gift.

"I almost forgot," he said. "Close your eyes and hold out your hands."

She obliged, giggling. Frank pulled the wrapped book from his coat pocket and set it into her outstretched hands.

"Okay, open them!"

"Frank! This is so nice!" She gave it a little shake. "Can I open it?"

"Sure."

As the front cover came into view, she gasped. Then she looked at him, tears in her eyes. "You're not going to believe this, but I lost my copy of this book a few months back. It's one of my favorites, but I hadn't gotten around to getting another one yet."

"Somehow, I'm not surprised," Frank said, taking her hand on purpose this time across the table.

11:00pm, December 25th, Christmas night

Shirley invited Frank to Christmas dinner at her house. To say he had enjoyed the meal with her and Liz and three other people was an understatement. He felt more at home the first time in Shirley's house than any other place he had lived. He didn't even have to ask where the bathroom was.

Shirley's friends, a married couple, Oscar and Theresa, and a young woman, Marley, not related, also felt like old friends. Liz, of course, had touched his soul the first time he cast eyes on her. Sharing Christmas with her was a delight.

After dinner, they all sat and talked for another two hours. And they made plans to get together the next day for breakfast at the diner.

Frank slept like the dead that night. No nightmares. No insomnia. No headaches.

The next morning, 6am sharp, Frank stepped out his apartment door. He wasn't surprised to see Liz standing there. He gave her a kiss on the cheek, and they walked, hand in hand, to the Geneva Towne Diner.

Oscar, Theresa, and Marley stood right inside the door, waiting for them. Frank was surprised to see the diner was almost full. He assumed people would be home with their families.

Families. He had forgotten to call his father to wish him a Happy

Christmas. Before he could think about that, two young women came up to their table.

"Can we join you?" the brunette asked.

"Sure!" Liz exclaimed. "Have we met before?"

"I don't think so. My name is Deb, and this is Michelle," the brunette said.

They all mumbled greetings as the waitress brought two more place settings. After placing their order, they sat sipping coffee. Finally, Deb broke the silence.

"You all are going to think we've gone off the deep end. I mean, we're total strangers, right? But Michelle saw you first, and we both felt drawn to you."

Michelle nodded. "Almost like we were compelled to come and sit with you."

"I gotta say, we're a bit freaked out," Deb continued. "We never had this happen before."

Frank shifted in his seat. They might be freaked out, but he was, too.

As if she heard his thoughts, Liz grabbed his hand and squeezed it tight. "We don't think you're crazy. Oscar, Theresa, and Marley had Christmas dinner with us last night. They just showed up at my mom's house."

Frank started. "Just showed up? I thought they were your mom's friends."

"Compelled," Marley whispered. "That's the word. We didn't even think about it. We just came."

Oscar leaned forward. "Theresa and I picked up Marley on our way to Geneva. I *never* pick up strangers. But I somehow knew her."

"We've never even *been* to Geneva," Theresa added. "But Oscar kept dreaming about it. The town and all. Shirley's bakery. What's it called again?"

"Shirley's Sweeties," Liz said.

"And I somehow knew which house was hers," Oscar said.

Frank held up a hand. "Wait—" he started. Then he looked at his hand. Which once again was not his hand.

He stared at it.

"Are you okay?" Theresa asked.

The words would not come out of his mouth. They couldn't. It wasn't his mouth.

"Frank? Hey, buddy," Oscar said. "Come on now. It's okay."

Marley started to cry. Theresa put an arm around her. The waitress came up with the coffeepot and Liz waved her away.

"Give us a few," she said. She touched Frank's shoulder and he slowly put his/not-his hand down. "It's okay. Breathe."

Frank took a shallow breath. Then he took a deeper one.

"Frank sometimes thinks his hands or other body parts are not his," Liz explained to Deb and Michelle, who were looking as though they had just ridden an out-of-control roller coaster.

Marley cried harder. Theresa hugged her close and explained, "Marley has had the same experience."

Michelle wiped her mouth with a napkin. "I have memories that aren't mine sometimes." She shrugged. "At least it feels that way. Like when you have a dream that feels real, but then you wake up and know it was a dream."

"Except you weren't sleeping," Deb said. "Same for me."

"I'm with Frank, as well," she added. "My hands, feet, and even my teeth don't feel like mine most days."

"Theresa and I don't have children," Oscar glanced at Theresa. "But there are times when we both wonder where our kids are."

They all sat quietly for a minute. Then Marley blew her nose and stuffed the tissue into her purse. "That leaves you, Liz. What's your story?"

Liz took a deep breath. She held it for about five seconds and blew it out. "I can't put my finger on it. Memory blanks. Memories that aren't mine. People I feel I know but have never met." She smiled. "Like Frank."

The waitress came over and refilled their coffee and water. Oscar asked for a slice of pumpkin pie, which made everyone chuckle. "I eat pie when I'm stressed," he said. And everyone laughed again.

"What do we do now?" Theresa asked. "We can't just go back home. It's about a two-day drive."

"What are our options?" Marley asked.

Frank *knew* he had to offer his place. "You can all stay with me. The apartment above the store is really quite big."

"Wow, thanks, Frank," Oscar exclaimed.

"Don't thank me yet," he said. "We're going to have to get creative for sleeping arrangements. I have a double bed in my room, a couch and recliner in the living room, and the other two bedrooms are empty."

"Michelle and I have a tent and two blow-up mattresses," Deb said. "We've been traveling for a while and money is tight. So, we've been staying in campgrounds or even fields if we can't find any place to stay."

"And freezing our butts off!" Michelle added.

Liz squeezed Frank's hand. "Thanks for offering, Frank. There's not much room in Shirley's house for sleeping."

Frank and the group headed for his apartment where they spent the day together, moving furniture, blowing up the air mattresses, and getting to know each other better.

After having pizza delivered for dinner, they agreed they'd meet at

Shirley's Sweeties for breakfast.

"Maybe Shirley can help us figure all this out," Frank said.

After Liz got a cab home and the others were settled, Frank went to his room and tried to go to sleep. But his thoughts plagued him, and no sleep came. When he was still staring at his alarm clock at 2:00am, he got up and went to the kitchen. He had Shirley's chocolate chip cookies in mind.

He had only eaten half a cookie when he got an overwhelming desire to *see* Shirley. To thank her for such delicious cookies. Right then. He thought he had shaken it off, but suddenly he was outside and walking. He wasn't even wearing a coat!

As he approached Shirley's house, he heard footsteps behind him. Without turning around, he knew it was everyone else. Oscar, Theresa, Marley, Deb, and Michelle.

No one said a word as they walked up the sidewalk to the front door.

Frank lifted a hand to knock, but the door opened.

"I knew you were coming," Liz said.

Still, no one spoke as they filed into the house. The living room was dark, so Liz went around the room and turned on the lamps. Then she came and stood next to Frank, taking his hand, and holding it gently.

Everyone took in an expectant breath.

Just then, Shirley came into the room wearing green surgical scrubs. She looked them all over with a big smile that made Frank feel uncomfortable.

"Hello, my sweeties! Time for your *fix and refresh*!"

The End

THE FEAR OF A MONSTER
Lindsi McIntyre

Alasi ducked through the hanging pelts that covered the front entrance. Father screamed profanities into the night at her back. Light poured out behind, casting her shadow across the ice-covered ground at her feet. Something slammed into her shoulder, hard but with a distinctive squish to it. Father complained constantly about his job fishing, so Alasi always wondered why he used his hard-earned spoils as weapons.

"Get out of my sight, you useless girl. Get out and don't come back. I don't care if you freeze to death."

His words struck harder than the fish and rent like knives through her heart. Alasi could only hope the early sunset and quickly dropping temperatures kept her neighbors from hearing. Their presence would serve no purpose. Alasi had learned early on that the others couldn't or wouldn't do anything to temper Father's abuse.

Making an oar-straight path for the tree line, she let the darkness of the forest engulf her, hide her from the shame and pain of Father's rage. The air bit at the exposed part of her face. Cold, but not nearly as cold as the way Father looked at her most days. She'd never understood that look in his eyes. Had given up trying long ago.

Now, she just tried not to provoke him too often.

The night lay still, save for the occasional bark of a white fox or howl of a distant wolf. Most creatures were smart enough to have tucked themselves away early to avoid the rapidly freezing air. Soon, even the foxes and wolves would return to their dens to avoid the coldest part of the long winter night.

Alasi would love to turn back as well, settle in by the warmth of the fire, but she had to wait for Father to drink himself to sleep.

Only then would it be safe.

The well-worn hunting path wound deep into the forest, but Alasi turned off into a small grove of trees after only a few yards. A log rested at the base of two large pines, shielded somewhat from the wind. A fine layer of snow glittered on the dark wood. The scene was still, peaceful.

Out here, she could almost forget.

With a sigh, Alasi pulled off the faded fur-lined leather glove on her right hand. The snow stung her palm as she brushed it away from the log. With a vicious shake, she knocked the painful remnant of frost from her fingers before forcing the affronted appendage back into the warmth of her glove. The momentary pain of touching the snow was preferable to the permanent pain of a soaked and frozen glove.

Alasi sat in the dark, surrounded by silence, interrupted only by the howl of wolves and the occasional crunch of snow falling in batches from trees overladen by its weight. Yet, despite the physical reprieve of the silence, Father's words still echoed, filling her chest with a crushing weight that had her wrapping her arms around her chest in a useless bid to ease the burden.

A twig snapped at her back, drawing her around sharply.

Surprised eyes that shone like stars stared out at her from a human face paler than snow.

Terror settled deep inside.

It was the monster.

Everyone knew the tale of the man-shaped creature Elder Kunkut had unknowingly brought in from the sea on his fishing boat. The old man's eyes hadn't seen clearly for decades, so the monster easily fooled him. Once on shore, others had warned the elder. The creature had fled into the forest surrounding their village.

Since then, horrible stories would surface of someone seeing the beast. Of being killed because they'd seen it.

Alasi could not believe her rotten luck. Why would the monster show up at her secret spot? It wasn't fair. She shouldn't have to die just because she'd seen—

But what if she hadn't seen it?

Her panicked mind latched onto the question. It was a mad, desperate ploy but if it worked…

"Who's there?"

The dead-eyed look she forced onto her face felt unnatural when every instinct in her screamed to hold the monster center in her gaze. She couldn't risk her eyes holding any focus if there was even a chance of success. Her voice quivered. She hoped it would think she was afraid because she *couldn't* see it.

It visibly relaxed as it caught on to her implied disability. The hand holding a walking stick by its side loosened its grip. Alasi felt more than saw the creature take her in, assessing her as a potential threat. She did her best to seem as small as possible.

Finally satisfied, the monster spoke. "What are you doing out here?"

The sound of his voice was different than her people's, but it seemed human enough. No wonder Kunkut had been fooled.

"Are you lost?"

Alasi blinked in surprise. That it would care seemed impossible. "N-no."

"Are you alone?" Those eyes searched the neighboring trees.

She realized it didn't care about her. It was worried others would see.

"Y-yes," she said, wishing she could say no.

"Why?"

"Oh. Well. I just—needed some air."

He shifted anxiously, continuing to peer between her and the trees surrounding her. He didn't believe her. And if he didn't believe her about that, he might start to question her ruse.

"Father—you see. Well, he—likes to be alone—when he drinks..." The flash of pity on his face drew her full focus. She hung her head. even knowing her reaction might cause him to realize the truth. He didn't seem to notice.

"Do you come out here often?"

There was more to his question than the words, but the truth served her purpose so she decided to tell it. He would never believe a blind woman had found a comfortable place on a trail alone, but she needed a natural way to bring it up. "Yes. I used to come out here with my mother when I was a child. I just follow the same path, now that she's gone."

The tightness in her chest threatened to move to her throat, so she changed the subject. "Why are you out so late?"

He peered out at the forest, this time in contemplation. "I'm not from around here. My presence tends to make people...uncomfortable. It's best if I check my traps at night. So I don't disturb anyone.

"And I like the night," he added. "It's calm. Makes it easy to forget...things."

She didn't know how to respond to that. The wind picked up. Alasi shivered hard despite her thick fur coat.

"A storm's rolling in. You had best be getting back to your home." He stood watching, as if waiting to prove she'd been lying.

Alasi swallowed hard and stood. This would be the ultimate test. One misstep, and he would catch on to her.

With falsely halting steps, Alasi made her way back to the path. She had to pass the monster, and she fought the urge to shrug away from him, knowing the action would give her away. He pulled back, letting her pass. She was about to breath a sigh of relief when the sound of his steps crushing snow followed.

He was keeping pace with her!

Why? Was he so intent on finding her out?

Alasi bit back her panic and focused on keeping her steps uncertain. It wasn't difficult. Her whole body shook from the building terror pounding through her veins.

Finally, the hut she shared with Father came into view. She'd never been so happy to see the tiny structure in her life. Alasi passed out of the tree line. The monster's footsteps stopped. Relief nearly knocked her to the ground, but she forced herself to keep moving. Past the overturned canoe Father took out on the mornings he wasn't too hung over. Past the lines where she hung their drying clothes. Past the fish Father had thrown at her back, its half-eaten remnants now frozen to the ground. Some white fox had gotten a good meal out of Father's temper.

With each step, her panic passed until her fear seemed foolish. The creature hadn't hurt her. Hadn't even raised its voice at her. Father had done far worse over the years, and yet she was practically running to get back into the same hut as him.

She suddenly wished she was back in the forest. That she had taken the chance to ask the monster more questions. Learn where it had come from. Why it had sailed in on the sea.

Pushing the fur covering the entrance aside, Alasi risked one last look at the beast. Only to find he'd already disappeared.

~~~~~

The woman was back.

Alasi.

For a moment, he just stared at her where she sat on the log in what had quickly become her spot in his mind.

This was the seventh night in a row she'd been waiting beneath the swaying pine branches that offered her at least some protection from the lightly falling snow. Each night, he expected to find her spot empty. Hoped she was safely tucked away in a bed by the fire.

Instead, she'd been out in the frozen wilderness.

Her father must be a brute of the worst sort. Gave his own real competition in the bad father race.

He stepped into her grove, sure to make enough sound that she wouldn't be afraid when he spoke. "Hello."

She turned, a hesitant smile on her lips. "Hello." Her unfocused gaze wavered in his general direction. "What would you like to talk about tonight?"

He smiled, the foreign tightness pulling at his cheeks. He hadn't had a lot of cause to smile in his life. "You tell me. You're the one with all the questions."

She laughed lightly and relaxed a bit. Each night she was a little quicker to let down her guard around him. He supposed meeting any strange man in the woods in the middle of the night would have caused the same reaction. He almost felt normal.

He joined her on the log. They sat in silence. He knew her well enough by now to know that meant her question was going to be a tough one to answer.

"Why don't you ever talk about your family?"

As he expected. How was he supposed to answer that? He sighed.
~~~~~

"There's nothing to talk about."

The silence stretched.

"I never knew my mother." Technically true. "And my father wanted nothing to do with me." He said the words with as little inflection as possible. Hoping she would believe he felt nothing when he said them. Wishing it were true.

She hung her head. "We're the same then."

Anger poured through his chest like fire. A familiar heat he'd hoped never to feel again. "No. We're not."

She flinched. He saw her chin wobble as she fought back tears at his sudden rejection. He rushed to reassure her. "Our fathers might have agreed neither of us were worth much. But my father was right. I'm the abomination he always said I was. *Your* father is just a drunk fool. You don't deserve to be treated the way he treats you."

Alasi turned toward him. She reached out to touch his face, and he flinched in response. "I think your father was wrong about you, too." Her touch was warm. It sent a pain through his chest that nearly doubled him over. But he didn't stop her. Shamelessly leaned into her palm with eyes shut.

She wouldn't say that if she could see him. If she knew what he was. It was only her blindness that protected him from the harsh reality of her hatred. But, in that moment, he could hope. He could dream. He could —

He opened his eyes and found her studying his face. He stilled as horror settled deep inside.

Alasi wasn't blind.

Her eyes widened as she realized she'd been caught. Fear tinged her gaze. She opened her mouth. To scream? He sprang to his feet, intent upon racing away.

"Wait," she cried out.

He kept moving.

Her hands latched around his arm. "Wait. Please, wait."

He wanted to fling her away but was afraid to hurt her. His strength was not something a true human could stand up against. "Let go."

"Please. Please stay."

He stared down at her in shock. "What?"

"Please stay. Don't go." Tears filled her eyes and slipped down her cheeks. "I don't want you to go."

"Are you mad?"

She blinked, freeing more tears.

He grabbed her upper arms and stared hard into her face. "Look at me. I'm a freak. A disgrace. A scourge on the earth."

"No. You're not." She shook her head furiously. "You're not. You're kind. And funny. And —"

He laughed. A dead sound that echoed through his dead heart. "Then why lie? Why pretend you couldn't see me? You knew what I was from the start. That's why you hid the truth." But that also meant she'd known who he was all those nights they'd spent talking. She had still come back to her spot. Had still asked her questions. Hadn't sent a horde of weapon-wielding villagers after his head.

"I was afraid," she muttered. "Because of the stories. But—it's different now."

His heart cried out, yearning for her words to be true. But they couldn't be. He couldn't let himself be fooled. "I have no place in the land of the living. Wanting one has only ever led me to pain." He wanted to laugh in derision, cry as a child abandoned. Instead, he decided to reveal the rest to her. Then she'd see.

"I've killed people. Innocent people. People whose only mistake was being somewhat related to the man who created me."

"Why?"

Where was the disgust he expected to see? "Because I was angry. Because—" He wasn't even sure he could explain what had gone through his mind back then. Certainly anger. But maybe more fear. As the truth of his existence had set in, he'd become desperate to escape his undead fate. The loneliness of his half life. And he'd been willing to sacrifice others to run from that fear.

She was watching him. Studying him. Her eyes filled with sadness. "That's what you've done. But it's not who you are."

He shook his head. "There's no difference."

"Yes, there is." Her fingers dug into his arms. "There is. You can change what you do whenever you want. Bring good into the world instead of bad. Help people instead of hurt them."

He thought of his father and the pain the man had inflicted on him during the first years of his life. He suspected she was doing the same.

"You can change."

He closed his eyes against the hope her words stirred.

Was it true? Could he ever be anything other than a monster?

"I don't know how," he replied on a breathless whisper.

"We can figure it out. Together."

He opened his eyes and watched a star shoot across the sky. He didn't know if she was right. Didn't know if he had any right to *wish* she were. But he did. He wished on that star with all his heart that this time, he could get it right.

"Okay."

The End

THE SENTINEL
Stoney M. Setzer

Everything looked familiar but different at the same time. He had been here at Janus Labs before, but it hadn't looked this way.

Memories rushed back to him. Sarge had talked about this, calling it Operation Breakout. Everybody else was in on it, Mays and Villanueva and Gillis. They had finally gone through with it, and they had all done this, trying to get away.

And that snake, Lockhart, is seeing everything I'm seeing. What if he uses me to track them down? I shouldn't be here...

The familiar pain erupted on either side of his neck. He tried to resist, but his willpower crumbled. A familiar voice went through his head, bypassing his ears. "Go inside, Boyle. You are our sentinel. That's all you're good for. Go in there and stand guard."

~~~~~

The five captives in the RV—all below the age of fifteen, each of different ethnicities—didn't know whether to be terrified or exuberant. Fear had been nothing new for them since they had been abducted, but this time their three captors weren't the reason.

Instead, it was the wolflike creature that had burst into the RV, standing on two legs like a man and wearing jeans and a t-shirt, albeit badly ripped. Already he had slaughtered two of the kidnappers and was working on the third. Beck, the others had called him. Beck had tried to shoot the wolf, but he would have accomplished just as much with a water pistol. The wolf pounced on him, yellow eyes gleaming, its snout going straight for Beck's throat...

They all looked away, but the sounds of ripping flesh and Beck's gurgled last breaths told them all they needed to know. One girl screamed, and someone else vomited.

"Which one of you is Tamara?" a throaty voice growled a moment later.

As one, they turned to look at the wolf. Still standing like a man, he was breathing heavily as if from overexertion. One of his upper limbs, the right one, was horribly maimed. However, their attention was all riveted on its face, which suddenly looked less wolfen, but not quite human.

"Is one of you named Tamara?" he asked again.

One girl of about thirteen raised her hand as if she was in school. "I am."
~~~~~

Fury seemed to give way to compassion on the creature's face. "Your parents hired me to rescue you and anybody else I found." He waited for a moment and continued. "There's a cell phone on the dashboard. One of you needs to call 911. Tell them that you are at the campground off Highway 72. Can one of you do that?"

One of the older boys nodded. "I can."

"Good. Tell them that you were abducted by human traffickers and that they are all dead now. If they ask how, tell them that a wild animal broke in and killed them…but don't mention that the animal talked to you." Something like a smirk crossed the werewolf's face. "They'd have just a little trouble believing that."

"Uh, yeah. I get it."

"None of you tell them that part. I am going into the woods, but I will stay close until help arrives for you. Then I'll be gone for good. Is everybody clear on that?"

Five heads nodded.

"Thank you," Tamara whispered. A sentiment quickly echoed by the others.

The werewolf nodded and fled into the night, while the older boy hustled over to find the cell phone.

<div align="center">~~~~~</div>

True to his word, Marshall Ritch waited in the woods, in a perfect spot to observe the RV in stealth. Once the police showed up, he plunged deeper into the woods, until he could find a place to transform himself back into his fully human form. Making his way back to his own RV on the other end of the campground, through the woods, he fished a grape soda out of the cooler with his good arm and stared out into the night.

As always, he felt conflicted. For the umpteenth time, he thought about the wreck and wished that he had died with Lizzie. Instead, Dr. Lockhart had operated on him. Now he was a widower with a maimed arm—and the curse of werewolf transformations and bloodlust. He was a monster now, a killer, even taking it a step further by making himself into a hitman.

On the other hand, it was through that business he tried to find redemption. He had learned to channel his wolfish urges by targeting specific types of people, those who constituted a different brand of monster entirely. Tonight's special had been human traffickers, but child abusers, sex offenders, and drug pushers were also frequent targets. If he had to spill blood, at least he could take solace that it didn't come from the innocent. Even though he had killed three men tonight, he had rescued five kids in the process, not to mention an untold number of potential future victims.

Sometimes he wondered if this ongoing quandary would push him to the outer limits of his sanity. *What if Lizzie could see me now? Can she see me from where she is? If so, do I look like a monster or an avenger?*

Either way, I never asked for this life. Not as a werewolf, and certainly not without her. I never would have wanted Dr. Lockhart to do this to me, and there's no telling how many other lives he has ruined. Surely I'm not the only one.

His search for answers was why he had happened to be passing through northern Mississippi when a former client had put Tamara's parents in contact with him. He was on his way back home to Sardis County, Tennessee. Back to where Dr. Lockhart had started him on this path.

Back to take out perhaps the biggest human monster of them all.

~~~~~

The RV park where he had rescued the kids was about two hours from Memphis, which itself sprawled about thirty miles west of Sardis. As always, Ritch had his yacht rock playlist going as he drove along. By the time he reached the Tennessee line, Toto was singing about not holding somebody back, and the irony brought a tear to his eye. Toto had been one of Lizzie's favorites, and this had been one of her favorite songs. With a little imagination, he could almost see her in the passenger seat next to him, singing along, her reddish-brown hair bouncing as her head bobbed to the beat. Just like she had been doing when Drunken Duncan staggered out in front of them, forcing Ritch to swerve and lose control...

Come on, Marshall. Focus.

He turned off the main highway just before he came to Memphis, veering northeast toward his former hometown. Driving one-handed wasn't easy to begin with, and now his trembling made it even more challenging. In a very short time—almost too short—he had crossed into Tennessee and saw the old sign: **Welcome To Sardis County. Dane M. Carter, Sheriff. Home Of The Bees, 1994 Tennessee High School Baseball Champs.**

Ritch hadn't been back to his old hometown since he had been released from the hospital. As much as he dreaded seeing the hospital again, making it his first stop in his search for Lockhart seemed logical. Sardis County didn't seem to have changed much, and he was able to navigate the familiar streets with ease. Soon he was pulling into the parking lot of a blockish three-story white building: Bloom Memorial Hospital. Often the locals referred to it as Doom Memorial because of all the patients who died there. Lizzie had been one of those, and Ritch often wished that he had been.

He parked in a remote corner of the lot and pulled out his cell phone. A quick check of the hospital's website produced a physician's directory, but Lockhart's name was nowhere to be found.

Maybe he doesn't work here anymore, but I wonder if anybody working here
~~~~~

knows where he went, Ritch thought as he tapped the link for the phone number. Fifteen minutes of wandering through a labyrinth of automated menus and endless hold music finally prompted him to end the call with a growl.

Going inside the hospital was a last resort. As soon as the automatic doors slid open in front of him, memories flooded his mind. Lizzie wasn't the only one who had breathed her last here; both of his parents had as well. Different circumstances, more natural causes, but they inspired painful memories, nevertheless. Struggling to keep his emotions in check, he strode to the information desk.

"Is Dr. Lockhart available?"

The smile on the young receptionist's face faltered noticeably. "I'm sorry, sir. Dr. Lockhart isn't here."

"Do you know when he will be back?"

"He won't be," a dark-skinned lady interjected as she stepped up beside the receptionist. "Dr. Lockhart is no longer affiliated with this hospital, and he is no longer allowed on this campus. I'm sorry if he's a friend of yours, but I hope to never lay eyes on him again."

Friend? Are you kidding me? Ritch hadn't expected this reaction, but he also couldn't blame them. Lockhart didn't need another chance to do this to anyone else. "What happened?"

"I'm afraid that I'm not at liberty to say. None of us are." The lady crossed her arms and looked him straight in the eye.

"Do you know where I can find him, at least?"

"I said, we're not at liberty…"

"Actually, young man, I believe I can help you," another voice said from behind him.

Ritch turned to see an old woman in a candy striper's uniform smiling at him. She was short and stout, creating the illusion that she was as wide as she was tall. "You're looking for Dr. Lockhart, you said?"

"Mrs. Dell!" the dark-skinned lady snapped. "No one here is allowed to discuss him!"

"But I'm not an employee here, Mrs. Tinsley," Mrs. Dell said sweetly. "I'm just a volunteer, and I can always leave and volunteer elsewhere. Come outside with me, sir, and let's talk."

Ritch followed her as she waddled through the nearest set of double doors, acutely aware of Mrs. Tinsley's gaze. Mrs. Dell found a bench and plopped down on it, patting one end in invitation. Hesitantly Ritch sat down.

"So, if you're here to see Dr. Lockhart, I'm guessing it's not a friendly visit," she said. "Just like I don't suppose you're likely to tell me your real name if I ask."

Ritch was too stunned to be pretentious. "How did you guess?"

She gave a half-smile. "I've known too many people like Dr. Lockhart. People who would use and hurt anyone for the sake of their own agenda. Anyone looking for the likes of him comes with revenge in their heart and a desire to seek it in secrecy."

"You're astonishingly perceptive. Now, you said you could help me?"

She looked him straight in the eye. "Are you familiar with these parts?"

"Yes ma'am, lived here most of my life until…well, you know. Lockhart."

She nodded. "I know indeed, sadly. Anyway, there is a place on the other side of the county, well outside the city limits, called Janus Labs. Do you know it?"

"I've heard of it, but that's about it."

Mrs. Dell pulled out a pen and an old receipt and scribbled down an address. "Last I heard, he went to work there after he was drummed out of here. If you don't find him, I'm sure you'll find something noteworthy, something enlightening."

"Great, thank you!" Ritch took the paper and hustled toward the parking lot.

Mrs. Dell sat there watching him for a full minute before she stood.

Mrs. Tinsley came outside and walked toward her. "Are you sure that was wise, Mrs. Dell? You know he's going to head out there now."

"I'm afraid so. But something tells me that there is more than meets the eye with him."

"You think he might possibly be of help to us?"

Mrs. Dell nodded. "Hopefully. May he be under God's protection," she said softly. "He's going to need it…just as we are going to need him."

~~~~~

Ritch drove through town, doing his best to keep his speed down. The route that the GPS plotted turned out to be a cruise down memory lane. He saw the defunct textile mills, buildings that should have been demolished long ago but now stood as architectural fossils. Walmart was still there, of course, with the IHOP situated toward the front end of the parking lot. In between them was still the vacant space where the second-rate summer carnivals set up shop.

Memories tugged hard at him as he passed Shiloh Baptist Church, where he and Lizzie used to be active members. She worked with the preschoolers, while he taught middle school boys in Sunday school — a lifetime ago, it seemed. A block away sat Memorial Park, the oddity that could only happen in Sardis County. Where else could anybody find a kids' playground right next to a cemetery…

…The cemetery where Lizzie was interred.
~~~~~

Ritch wanted to stop, but he found a plethora of excuses to keep on driving. The layout of the parking lot was anything but RV-friendly. Driving the RV made him conspicuous enough and trying to pull into a place like Memorial Park would only draw more attention. Attention was the last thing he needed. At least until he had accomplished his mission.

Maybe he could park elsewhere later and come back on foot, after he was finished with Lockhart. Should he be successful, then visiting her grave would seem like the perfect closure. If that didn't go well, for whatever reason, he might find himself near her anyway—in the ground beside her.

~~~~~

Reject. How many times have I been called that?

Back in school, coaches always wanted Boyle on their teams because he was a big guy, but he wasn't good enough to play much. His grades weren't necessarily bad, but they certainly weren't good enough to gain him any kind of special recognition. As for the girls, striking out was practically a given.

Even now, after his National Guard squadron had been abducted and experimented on, he was still an outcast. He and another soldier had been spirited away from the lab for some kind of special experimentation before Sarge and the others tried to escape, so he missed out on that. Then the other guy was considered more successful, so he got all the attention.

Meanwhile, I get sent back to be the sentinel over a graveyard. All because I'm not good enough…and it's not like I'm going to fit in anywhere else, not after what they've done to me.

Every muscle in his body tensed as he saw movement on one of the security monitors.

But who would come here?

The pain on either side of his neck told him that he wasn't the only one who had seen it.

~~~~~

"You've arrived," the GPS voice announced as Ritch pulled up to a brick fence with an iron gate, sitting out in the middle of nowhere. An unmanned guard shack sat just to the left of the entrance lane.

"Figures," he muttered as he put the RV in park. Never having seen Janus Labs before, Ritch didn't know what to expect, but he wasn't surprised that it would be a secure facility, unobservable from the road. The lack of a security guard on duty was surprising, however, even a little disconcerting. *Why isn't there anybody on duty?*

Inside the guard shack was a broken coffee cup with a dried puddle of what must have once been coffee with creamer, flanked by an old, half-eaten blueberry doughnut. A library copy of a Dean Koontz novel, *Prodigal Son*, lay haphazardly on the floor, either thrown down or dropped. Ritch frowned.

The control panel was straightforward enough, with the button to open the gate clearly labeled. He reached for it and then paused, mulling his options. Ritch had learned how to transform on his own, independently of the full moon. He was tempted to do so now and enter on foot, but he decided against it. Better to stay in human form for now, drive in, and then transform when he had Lockhart in his sights. Under ordinary circumstances, he might have been concerned about the RV being too conspicuous, but the abandoned guard shack suggested that might not be a problem—and that there might be bigger things to worry about.

Beyond the gate, there was nothing but empty acreage as far as the eye could see. A weathered driveway stretched straight ahead, eventually disappearing over the top of a hill. Ritch followed the path, scanning the landscape around him. The tableau was too quiet for his liking. Something happened to make the sentry abandon his post, and it had happened long enough ago for the spilled coffee to dry completely. And nobody, neither the guard nor anybody else, had been back to clean up the mess.

As Ritch drove further, a barrage of odors assaulted his nose. One of the side effects of his lycanthropy was his heightened sense of smell, now that of a wolf even when he was in human form. He could make out the residue of a number of different burnt items somewhere up ahead, probably beyond the ridge. Most disturbing, however, was the distinctive stench of putrefying corpses—several of them, all deceased long enough to reek. Fighting down apprehension and nausea, Ritch continued forward, up to the top of the hill.

Once he could see the other side, the scene at the guard shack and the smells made more sense. He felt as if he was looking down at a war zone. There were at least twenty buildings of varying sizes down below, and almost all had sustained significant damage. Some had burned, others had not, but none of them seemed fully intact. Across the way was another hill, then a brick fence with a substantial hole knocked out of it, big enough for Ritch to see a set of old, overgrown railroad tracks beyond it.

Most telling, however, were the bodies. Thirty or so corpses were strewn on the ground in random spots, much like one might expect to see on a battlefield. Even from this distance, Ritch could tell that their deaths had been brutal. Some of them had been killed in explosions, others had been burned, and still others had been crushed by heavy objects.

A few of the deceased wore outfits that looked like gray jumpsuits, making him wonder if they might have been the subjects of experiments. Several more sported the uniforms of security guards. There were also a few white lab coats among the deceased, catching Ritch's attention. Could Lockhart have been among them?

Would I even want *Lockhart to be among them? Do I want somebody else getting to him first? If all I want is vengeance, maybe not. But if I want a cure…*

Wait! What was that?

Ritch froze in his tracks, listening intently for several moments. He was just about to write it off as a figment of his imagination when he heard it again. A footstep. Somewhere down there in all that rubble, somebody was moving. Somebody was alive.

He made his way down the hill on foot. If that survivor was an innocent victim of some experiment, they needed help. And if the survivor just happened to be Lockhart, he needed something else entirely.

~~~~~

"You must attack the intruders. You must kill them."

Boyle shook his head. "No, I don't want to…"

"You must. You have no choice."

The neck pain intensified, nearly drowning out Boyle's thoughts…

~~~~~

A sense of danger charged the air itself. The carnage made it obvious, but there was something else there, something that went beyond what ordinary human senses could have perceived. If Ritch had been in his werewolf state, the hairs on his back would have been standing on end. He stayed as quiet as possible as he descended the hill, careful not to signal his arrival until he could tell whether the survivor was a threat.

Stealth would have been easier in his werewolf state, but he forced himself to stay in human form. Only having one good arm wasn't ideal if a physical confrontation arose, but he could always transform if something happened. Holding off gave him the element of surprise, more than adequate compensation for his mangled right arm.

Now that he had a closer vantage point, Ritch tried to visualize the scene. The bricks from one of the devastated walls lay scattered outside its building, suggesting that it had been smashed from the inside. If the experiments conducted here were anything like what Lockhart had done to him, then this was probably an escape attempt. The subjects must have been working together to cause this much damage, suggesting an organized attack. He doubted that the number of men he saw in gray jumpsuits could have done all this. There must have been more, and judging from the hole in the fence, some of them had gotten away.

He knelt by some of the bodies to examine them more closely. None of them showed any fang or claw marks—no signs of a werewolf attack. If one of the escapees had lycanthropy and could control the transformations like Ritch could, then surely he would have tried to fight as a wolf rather than as a man. What other kinds of experiments had Lockhart been doing on these people?

Ritch wasn't sure he wanted to know.

Sniffing the air frequently and listening intently, he made his way through the debris, looking for whoever he had heard. The sounds still came intermittently, but it was hard to pinpoint their source. He hoped to catch a whiff of live flesh somewhere. Finding nothing out in the open, he would have to check the buildings one at a time.

The nearest building was a charred hull with a sign reading GENETICS. A thorough search yielded nothing. Slowly, systemically, he made his way to the next one.

~~~~~

Closer, closer. Too close. He will find me soon, and then Lockhart will force me to…

"Be ready to attack, Boyle. No one must know about you or this place…"

~~~~~

Eureka, Ritch thought.

Inside the third building, the live flesh scent was more evident. Not exactly strong, suggesting that the source was in a different room or perhaps another floor altogether — except this was a one-story building. Cautiously, Ritch moved from one room to another, checking thoroughly. He found nothing, yet the scent was undeniable. The sounds were gone now, as if whoever had made them was now very still.

This can't be everything. Could I have missed a room somewhere?

He backtracked, scanning every inch of the walls. Having tried every door he saw, he now wondered if there might be a secret door somewhere. At last, he spotted it. In the men's restroom, there was a large space of open floor where the tile pattern matched everything around it, except for a barely visible seam outlining one section.

Now he just had to figure out how to open it. He groped along the restroom walls, hoping to find some kind of a trigger. After probing every square inch of the bricks, he moved on to the fixtures. On the underside of the sink, he felt a tiny button and pressed it. The section of tile slid open with a pneumatic hiss, revealing a spiral staircase beneath it.

Once that was opened, the smell of live flesh was more discernible, as were the sounds of movement. Ritch hesitated. There was no telling what sort of danger might await him down there, but he couldn't shake the idea of an innocent survivor, in trouble and in need of rescue. His only hope for redemption hinged on helping the innocent.

"Lord, if You still listen to me after all I've done, please help me," he prayed under his breath before starting down the stairs.

~~~~~

A few track lights still functioned, just enough to prevent the shadows from completely engulfing the secret room. Ritch considered using the flashlight on his cell phone but quickly nixed the idea. With only
~~~~~

one functioning arm, he had to be very intentional about how he used it. As much as the flashlight would have helped, he wanted his good arm free.

The secret room reminded Ritch of a fallout shelter. Shelves loaded with supplies and canned goods lined the concrete walls. A few gaps on the shelves indicated that someone had been making use of the reserves. Ritch sniffed the air. The smell of life was stronger than ever, but he also noticed that some kind of air filtration system was still at work. Maybe the air wasn't the freshest, but it hadn't gone completely stale, and there was surprisingly little dust. Whoever was down here couldn't have been here very long. Listening closely, he could make out the sounds of a generator, maybe not functioning at peak efficiency, but still operational…

…And something else. A snarl, low and guttural. Threatening, full of warning and bridled fury.

Ritch whirled around to see a hulking form standing just inside the shadows. His head missed scraping the ceiling by mere inches. A body cam was strapped onto his chest. On either side of his neck was a small, dimly luminous nub. He reminded Ritch of Frankenstein's monster, complete with bolts on his neck. The behemoth snarled again, louder. It didn't take much imagination to grasp the intent: *Get out of here.*

"Well, well, if it isn't Marshall Ritch! What a surprise!"

Ritch recognized the voice immediately as the hairs on his neck stood on end. He looked around in the darkness. "Lockhart! Where are you? Show yourself!"

Dr. Lockhart laughed. "Miles away from you, Ritch. Technology is a marvelous thing. By the way, welcome home."

"Home? I've never been here in my life!"

"I meant Sardis County as a whole, not Janus Labs. You were one of my field experiments, back when you were at Doom Memorial after your unfortunate accident. Right now, you are at the hub, my former headquarters, if you will."

"And where are you?" Ritch demanded, careful to keep an eye on the behemoth.

"Now if I told you that, you might be tempted to hunt me down, which I'm sure is how you found yourself in my old lab right now. Assuming, of course, that you survive Mr. Boyle here. Take a good look at him, Marshall. He makes you obsolete."

The lights brightened, causing Ritch to instinctively shield his eyes. As they adjusted, he saw just how apt the Frankenstein comparison was. Boyle stood around seven feet tall, plus or minus a few inches, and was built like a rhinoceros. His skin had a deathly pallor, almost but not quite gray, and looked as if it had been grafted together in numerous places. A pair of beady eyes were locked on him but had a glazed quality. The protrusions on his neck looked like metallic bulbs of some sort, further driving home the monster image.

"Quite an impressive specimen, isn't he?" Lockhart asked. "We had conscripted a National Guard squadron to help us with our experiments. As was the case with you, we introduced quantities of caprinium into their bloodstreams…"

"Caprinium? What is that?"

"That would be the element that made you what you are today. With each subject, it produces both a disability and a superhuman ability, only we can't predict what those manifestations will be."

"So my arm has nothing to do with the wreck," Ritch said.

"It was broken, but it would have healed normally in time — well, minus the fact that you were at death's door when I operated on you. With the addition of caprinium, it withered, but then you gained the ability to transform into a werewolf — probably at will by now."

"What about him?"

"Boyle here was one of several whom we took off-campus for experiments. Superhuman strength, but in several places his skin was, shall we say, missing — so we had to graft skin from cadavers until his epidermis was almost a patchwork quilt. We wanted the strongest, but there were some even stronger than him who were of more use to us. So I sent him back to act as a sentinel to guard this place."

"Why would you need a guard here?"

"All of the members of his squadron were affected differently. You should have seen it. We had a blind telekinetic, an acromegalic fire-starter, all sorts of combinations. Eventually the squadron combined their forces and escaped. I sent Boyle here in case any of them ever tried to come back — or in case anyone else tried to find out what we were doing here."

"So all that up above, that was from them joining forces to bust out of here?"

"Exactly. Glad to see that caprinium had no adverse effects on your brain."

Yeah, except for having to find ways to channel this urge to kill. "Why are you doing this?"

Lockhart's tone became more somber. "A threat is out there — a living nightmare. Our conventional military is powerless against it. We need something more, warriors to stand against—"

"I don't want any part of it," Ritch interrupted. "I never asked you to save my life, and I certainly never signed on to be a guinea pig or a warrior or anything else."

"Yes, I was afraid that you might feel that way if ever our paths crossed again. As disappointing as it might be, I can grant your wish." Lockhart cleared his throat. "Boyle, attack the man in front of you. Kill him."

~~~~~

No, no, it's wrong, I don't want to...
"Kill him!"

~~~~~

Please, God, no. There's only one way I can fight this man, and I don't want...

The neck bulbs flashed. With startling speed, the giant lunged forward, growling in savage fury. Ritch rolled to his left, narrowly escaping.

Boyle charged again as Ritch tried to stand. Unable to get clear, Ritch threw up a leg and tripped him, sending him sprawling. The impact with the floor stunned Boyle for a moment—all the time Ritch needed. *No holding back now.* He concentrated, focused on werewolf mode...

His teeth lengthened into fangs as his nails transformed into claws. Fur erupted across his flesh as his shirt ripped. Within seconds, he faced his assailant as a werewolf.

Boyle tried to stand as his neck bulbs flickered again. Ritch slammed into him from behind, knocking him back down. His claws ripped across Boyle's shoulder, drawing blood. Rolling off his target, Ritch held his claws up to his snout, sniffing the red fluid covering them. His werewolf thirst for blood would become urgent, but he was counting on it to help him survive.

Smell the blood. Get thirsty. No man, no monster, only hunter and prey and survival. Me or him.

The neck bulbs flashed again. Boyle rose quickly, just in time to meet Ritch's next attack. Like a thunderclap their impact boomed through the room.

Ritch was fighting two battles. Besides the behemoth, a war raged within him, man versus beast. His feral side wanted to rip Boyle's jugular out and be done with it. End it, quench the thirst, live to fight another day.

But he's human too, or at least he was. I didn't ask for this—maybe he didn't either. And he didn't attack me until Lockhart commanded—

A huge fist hammered into Ritch's jaw. It dazed him for a moment, and then animal fury took over. He sank his teeth into Boyle's upper arm and didn't let go, spurred on by his opponent's pained shouts. Not a killing move, but if he could do enough damage to take out that right hook...

Humanity began to reassert itself. *Can I survive without killing him?*

"Finish him, Boyle!" Lockhart commanded. "Your purpose is to kill your enemies! Kill him, already!"

Again the bulbs flashed.

They're connected, Ritch realized. *Every time Lockhart gives him a command, they flash.*

Boyle swung his arm, hurling Ritch against the wall. He leaned forward to keep his head from taking the brunt of the impact, but it knocked the wind out of him. As he sank to the floor, he felt the behemoth's footsteps shaking the room. Ritch rolled out of the way just in time to avoid a potentially devastating kick.

Can't just stay on defense. Got to mount some offense…

Boyle came again with surprising speed. Looking around, Ritch saw a nearby shelf loaded with canned goods. He struck it with his maimed arm, ignoring the pain. The shelf toppled over on Boyle, knocking him down and burying him under an avalanche of steel cans and wood. Beneath the pile, the behemoth lay motionless, stunned if not unconscious.

Acting quickly, Ritch scrambled over and clawed at one of the neck bolts, dislodging it quickly if not neatly. He lamented only having one good hand, otherwise he could have targeted both bolts at the same time. Boyle began to stir as Ritch started on the second bolt.

"Finish him!" Lockhart bellowed through the speakers.

Boyle rolled over with enough force to knock Ritch off balance. He raised one arm as if to strike, but the destructive rage had left his face.

"Get the other one," he said in an imploring voice. "Release me before he makes me kill you."

Clawing at the remaining bolt again and again, Ritch finally pulled it off and slung it across the room. Boyle dropped like a rock. Ritch watched him for several seconds, debating whether it was safe to revert to his human form.

At last Boyle opened his eyes. "I'm free. Thank you."

"What a pair of miserable failures," Lockhart said. "Fortunately, we have more successful test subjects elsewhere."

Ritch started transforming back. "You have no right to do this to people, Lockhart! I'll hunt you down if it's the last thing I ever do!"

"If you do, it truly will be the last thing you ever do, Marshall." A metallic click broke the connection.

"He's a menace," Boyle said. "We may look like monsters on the outside, but him…"

"I wonder what his game is," Ritch said. "He's got to have some bigger goal in mind."

They left the building and were walking through the battlefield when Boyle pointed to the top of the hill. "Who is that?"

Ritch did a doubletake. At the top of the hill, looking down on them, was the distinctive figure of Mrs. Dell. He hustled up the hill to her. "What are you doing here?"

"I had to see. I had to find out if you survived or not. Thank God, you have…and I see you found someone else who looks like they've had dealings with Lockhart."

Ritch's head was swimming. "Did you know about all this, Mrs. Dell?"

"I knew bad things had been done here, but no specifics. That was why I felt compelled to come out here and check on you."

"With no regard to your own safety?" Ritch tried to imagine her facing Boyle on her own.

She smiled. "I'm more capable than I might appear, and I've seen more than you can possibly imagine. Now that I see you have survived, I know that there is something special about you as well."

"I don't know that *special* is the word I'd use for it. More like *cursed*."

"No matter what you call it, I assure you that it is for a purpose, a larger one than you ever imagined. With that in mind, I have a proposition for you — and perhaps your friend here."

Ritch looked at Boyle and then back at her. "Proposition? What kind of a proposition?"

"I was wondering if you boys would be willing to help me," she said. "You see, Lockhart is just a cog in a bigger machine. I'm trying to organize a team — a team to help stand up against that greater threat. Are you interested?"

The End

THE MAN ON THE TRAIN
Abigail Falanga

12 July, 1945

Boarded train at D— Station. Package delivered. All well.

Can't be comfortable. War over in this part of the world, but only thing different is lack of shelling. Not quiet. Too many people—too much fear.

Later—

More got off at the last stop than got on; there's more room now. Found a spot to sit at one end of a bench. Almost comfortable. Could sleep. Will note what I see instead—best to keep awake.

Space is cluttered with goods, packages, luggage. Smells of refuse and sweat. Dark, but for small electric lights. Other side of car has two family groups—young children, some women, a couple of old folks. Poles, I think. American GIs playing cards on the floor. Old man on bench opposite me, near window. Been through a lot, to judge by his coat and trousers. Seems to be traveling alone. Afraid of something—keeps checking window every time we slow or stop.

Offered me a cigarette just now. American made. This old fellow is not what he seems, I think...

"*Anglais*?" he asked just now in an American accent.

I assent.

He nods thoughtfully, silent now. I wouldn't mind talk. Might keep my mind off... everything...

"Long way from home," I begin.

"So're you, son." He chuckles.

"I have assignments. But you—?"

"I..." He has a bitter smile in the light from his cigarette. "I am running for my life."

"Aren't we all?"

"Oh, it's quite literal in my case, I assure you. I don't have much time left, either. He'll catch up to me soon. Any time now, in fact. Still—I'm running away. If there's one thing this goddarn war has shown me, it's that I'm a coward. Can't face him and have it over with."

"Who?"

"My son. My creation." His exhale turns into a cough—the bad kind.

He's been hurt.

But I'm startled, nearly dropped my pen just now. Damn light in here.

He's talking now, a steady stream of words that won't stop even if I wanted it to. I'll take it down word for word as best I can, to keep awake...

It's still classified, I suppose, so I shouldn't share all this. But I've been carrying the weight a long time and a man's got to find relief somehow. Doesn't matter much anyway—the war's won, and we'll put all this behind us. Just do me a favor and tear out those pages and burn them when you get a chance, and forget I ever talked. You'll do that for me, son? Good.

Well, then...

I'm a scientist—a biologist. Back before all this started, I was at the forefront of glandular research, genetics, vivisection, eugenics. Improving the human race—that's what I wanted! We could do it, too. We made breakthroughs, let me tell you, some that will go on to impact the normal, everyday life of millions of people. Medicines that will prolong life. Vitamins and minerals and their impact.

What really interested me, though, was the idea of vastly improving the human body, mind, longevity, intelligence. Eugenics, now... There's a lot of potential in eugenics, but it's too darn slow! Think about it. Generations before a focused breeding program produces appreciable results, and even then, you can't be guaranteed the results you want. It's not like breeding dogs—humans take longer to reach maturity, and isolating qualities to enhance is not easy.

Hitler, now, made the mistake of discarding the unfit, whereas I always wanted to take the unfit and make them something more—something beyond the ordinary. Why waste what's there? Why even waste the dead? All we needed was the right resources, the facilities of time and money and space, and I was convinced that we could create the ultimate in humanity even from what society had discarded. The uber-man. Think about it!

That was where I was at the end of the last decade. But always—*always* I ran up against a lack of funding and the necessary collaboration. Futile moralistic scruples, or lack of vision. Then the war started, and suddenly it's in the country's best interest to have the best possible soldiers on the field and to field as many soldiers as they could. So, naturally, they turned to me, and other scientists in similar fields. Hacks, some of them, but it didn't matter because finally—*finally* I had the resources and facilities I had needed for so long.

Think about it. War breaking around us, and finally I had what I needed. Not just money, though there was plenty of that at first. Or space, since we were headquartered at a requisitioned hospital deep in the Nebraska flatlands. Nor even live volunteers, for we had those from the training soldiers at the base not far away. But *bodies*. That's what I had always needed! A source of fresh, reasonably intact corpses from fit young men. And war provided that.

What, does that horrify you?

Well, yes. I suppose it was… perhaps a little ghoulish.

But it was no worse than giving a wounded man a blood transfusion. Someday, our research might allow a new heart or kidney or lung to be grafted in to replace a damaged one. It's lifesaving, my boy — think of it! Taking viable tissue from the corpse of a boy who no longer needed it, to add to a boy who might be stronger and more perfect with it — that was what we were doing.

I had theorized and experimented on lab animals for years, of course, with a few small procedures on those ill to the point of death. So, when the opportunity arose, I was fairly certain of success. All I needed was a means of galvanizing the disparate parts into wholeness — more than wholeness. Greatness. Something *beyond*. More than the amphetamines, steroids, hormones — something more. This I found at last among a select few volunteer subjects.

You know the kind. That sort of person who is strangely capable in some area, beyond the ordinary. The ones who can hear extraordinarily well, or see spectrums of light beyond normal eyes, or yet more wondrous things than that. The kind who stepped up to fight this war and got slaughtered for their trouble. Well, my superiors went to the trouble to gather as many of these men as they could, and among them, I found my ways of joining parts into a whole.

My little lightning bolt, I like to call it.

Needn't tell you more than that. Suffice it to say…

I was ready.

Just needed the right volunteer to try it on.

Found him among the recruits in the bootcamp. Scrawny kid, hunched due to a congenital spinal condition, wheezing with asthma and some worse lung condition, poor eyesight… Don't know how he made it into the Marines, unless by sheer force of will. You could see it in his eyes — that passion to fight, to prove himself. Won't tell you his name. I always call him Adam, because he was my first creation.

The real reason he was there was that he was unusually gifted, like I was talking about just now. He could heal remarkably well, even though he was crippled in other respects — could recover from injuries in half the time it took ordinary men, unless he got one of those infections to which he was susceptible. That was the kind of thing my superiors were looking for, but even so, Adam might've been sent home on account of his handicaps if I hadn't found him.

I remember my first interview with him. Asked him why he thought himself capable of serving in the Marines, given his chronic conditions.

"I have to," he said.

"That's it?" I had to know. Get to the reason behind the passion that seemed to burn him up from inside.

"My father was in the Marines, and served with honor. My grandfather, too. My great-grandfather was killed at Gettysburg. My uncles have all served, and my younger brothers are planning to sign up as soon as they're old enough. You have to understand, sir, if I don't serve in the Marines, I'll let my whole family down. They already think I'm worthless. I have to prove to them that I'm man enough to fight, even if it kills me."

"That's the kind of drive I need," I said. "That won't-back-down spirit."

"I won't back down, sir." He almost yelled that. It made him cough so bad he had to sit down. When he recovered, he gave me a look that was all fear and desperation. "You're going to send me back home, aren't you, doctor? Or put me on a desk job?"

"No, son. I'm going to give you a chance. But you must know before you take it that it means an experiment so daring that it's never been tried before, it will involve grafting donor parts into your body to strengthen and transform you, and it is dangerous."

"I don't mind danger. And I'm used to pain." There was more than passion in his eyes now. There was hunger. He needed this. "I'll do anything."

It was his own choice, you see. He agreed to it.

The one thing I could have done was explain better. But even then... It *was* his choice.

The procedure was undertaken as soon as we reasonably could. My colleagues put more strictures in place as regards the patient's health and safety of the operations than I would have liked, though their caution may have been warranted since we needed success. Our superiors were as desirous of a good outcome as I was, or more.

Yet even they balked at the operations as they extended. They lasted several hours—more than a single day—and Adam was...

It wasn't...

We could not keep him under full sedation for certain parts of the procedure, since we needed full responsiveness to stimuli. The pain levels were... (interrupted by coughing fit) ...not fully anticipated, even by myself. Adam was in considerable pain throughout, and afterwards during recovery. At points he even begged...

Nevertheless, the procedures went well. There were few unforeseen complications, and these were well within my skill in overcoming. We began with a spinal operation, injecting —

Oh, I suppose you might not wish to hear these details.

No, no, it's all right. They may not be of interest to anyone not of scientific training. Moreover, yes, yes, I believe many of the details are still under strictest secrecy.

Very well, I will move on.

Recovery was protracted. It was not until a couple of months later that Adam regained full use of his limbs. He refused to speak to me during this time, so I only know from my attendants that the pain was slow to pass, but that in its place came strength such as he had never known before. Indeed — strength beyond anything seen in ordinary man.

We had succeeded!

Adam was no longer merely man, but *uber*-man. His height was full and straight, his strength was truly extraordinary, reflexes astounding, vision fully restored, stamina increased, healing beyond even what he'd possessed before. There was no sign of the lung disease that had beset him all his life. By every measurement, he was the very thing I had longed to create — the next stage in perfecting humanity!

I was overjoyed, and deeply hoped to celebrate with Adam himself. It was our shared triumph. He had wanted this as much as I did. Nearly as much as my superiors. They were desperate for this new weapon to send onto the battlefield.

As soon as Adam's attending doctors and nurses declared him healed enough, therefore, my superiors arranged that he be sent into specialized training — either back to the bootcamp, or somewhere else, I am not entirely sure which. It was too soon for me. I would have liked to run tests, examine the subject, extract samples... But I was not my own master any more than Adam was.

But one good thing came of it: Adam at last agreed to meet me. Demanded it, in fact.

So that night — the last before he was transferred — I went down the hall where drinks and *hors d'oeuvres* were served. It was our celebration at last. There was champagne, I remember. Someone put a glass into my hand, still frothing, and gave me a cigar.

Then I saw him...

I... must confess that I recoiled. Nearly turned and left. Yes... I was almost sick.

Adam was perfect. In every way. Tall and handsome, the image of the good American boy sickness and deformity had denied him. Stronger and wider. Without scar or blemish. The perfect human. The first. Even then, I meant him to be merely the first...

And yet...

In that first sight, would you believe he seemed more like a corpse than a man?

Perhaps it was only because I knew where I had gotten the material to rebuild him. Every fluid, sinew, tendon, organ, that I had taken and put together again within Adam seemed to have left a mark. His eyes were dead. But still they burned with a passion beyond even what he'd shown before.

A moment later, I told myself to stop being fanciful. It was strange, yes. But only in the way that utter physical transformation *is* strange. After all, one is repulsed when one encounters a friend who has lost all his teeth, or had his leg amputated, or…

Why do I say these things in terms of loss? It wasn't loss! It was gain. In every way, Adam was *more* than he had been before. He was greater, stronger, better!

It was merely a temporary repulsion. It passed…

Yet…

I knew in that instant that I had lost everything.

Adam was supposed to be my greatest creation. My son. The only son I would ever have. But there he was…

Regret? Regret creating him? Don't be crazy! Of course, I didn't regret! I'd do it again in an instant. The advances, the knowledge, the gains we made through that operation…! Are you crazy? Talking about regret…

I recoiled. It was a reflex. It passed.

But Adam saw.

He smiled at my entrance, but that smile twisted and turned sour. He hid it as quickly as I recovered my composure.

"Dr. Franklin!" he called as he spread out his arms wide. "Here it is! Look what you've made of me."

Everyone cheered and raised their glasses, myself included, toasting our success. We were giddy with it.

But he hadn't meant it as a declaration of victory or congratulations. I took it like that then — everyone did. Yet it was anything but, as I realized later.

It was an accusation.

That night, Adam was on top of the world, or seemed to be. He had finally gotten everything he wanted, and he said over and over how he was going to be the soldier that he'd always dreamed of being, make his family proud. You know how young men talk. Bluster and cockiness. By the end of that party, I was as happy for him as I would have been for my own son graduating college. That brief moment of horror was forgotten under a bottle of bubbly and a few cigars.

But he wasn't going to be some simple soldier. What idiot would waste a success like that by sending him to the front lines? Adam was shipped off with a special clandestine unit. I didn't know much about it, for security reasons obviously. And I didn't need to. That wasn't my department. I felt sorry for the boy, in a way. He'd wanted to serve in the field so badly, and then to have his very existence hidden under all those hush-hush operations… He saw action, of course. Guerilla stuff. That kind of thing.

And there I was, at home, with the best facility I'd ever had — tied up in red tape. They let me experiment and create new things, naturally. But the procedures on Adam had given my superiors the willies and they didn't have the guts to keep at it. I couldn't get approval to do more than the most basic operations, honing my little lightning-in-a-bottle to near perfection, but without any subjects to try it on beyond the smallest ways. Not on Adam's scale. I found this intensely frustrating even after I saw — him — what it had done to him.

Anyway, there I was, fighting that darn red tape for nearly a year. During that time, would you believe I fell in love and got married? I lost my first wife early, and after that was married to my job. But Elizabeth… she was something special. Rare beauty, salt of the earth. Smart as a whip, too, and could talk about research at the highest levels. She was a molecular biologist, you understand, doing studies in the facility that complemented my own. The only thing we ever seriously disagreed about was the end goals of my experiments — Elizabeth thought I was pushing boundaries I had no right to approach, which was ridiculous since I had already had success with Adam.

So, when Adam was transferred back to the base for a couple of weeks for tests, I invited him to come to our little place for dinner one night. I must confess, I hoped Elizabeth would be persuaded by the sight of him, my triumph, and use her influence to talk the honchos into approving further operations.

Adam had changed. Grown up, I thought at first. He wasn't a boy anymore. Well — that wasn't surprising, he'd seen war, that changes a man. But there was something else. His eyes didn't have that burning passion anymore — they'd hardened, so you couldn't tell what he was thinking or feeling. That only added to the first impression I had had looking at him that he was dead, which came back to me stronger than ever the longer he sat with us over the pork chops and beer.

He wasn't dead, of course. More alive than ever. Bigger, stronger, there wasn't an injury on him — not a mark, half-healed or scarred. And his hands… big and strong with the tendons I'd rebuilt, moving restlessly as if they remembered the men he'd killed.

Let me get another cigarette. Dropped mine…

Anyway, he was as polite as any good farm boy would be.

"Thanks for having me over, Mrs. Franklin," he said. "Good to have some home cooking for once."

"Don't mention it!" Elizabeth smiled politely, but then laughed. She had a lovely laugh, like a gentle rain. "Actually, I can't cook at all. It's disgraceful. Nearly burn the house down every time I try! No—Victor is responsible for these pork chops."

"Well, Dr. Franklin certainly knows how to cook." Adam grinned with everything but his eyes, and didn't look at me. "As I know from personal experience."

Somehow that made the whole room uncomfortable.

Elizabeth gave a little cough and changed the subject. "Have you made it back home to see your folks yet?"

"No." Adam shook his head, staring down at his plate. "Can't go home. Never again."

We talked about other things after that. Normal things. Don't even remember what. But after he left, while we were cleaning up and Elizabeth was washing dishes, she said something that shook me to the core, though I'd known it a long time:

"He hates you, you know."

"Don't know why!" I blustered at her. "I gave him what he wanted."

She shook her head, hands shaking so much she nearly dropped a plate. "He frightens me, Vick."

Ridiculous woman's fancies. I yelled at her. Turned it into our first big fight...

But she was right, as it turned out.

The second and last time Adam came back to the base, about six months later, he burned down my lab.

Not that we had any hard evidence, but everyone *knew*.

He was for in testing and to have further physical samples drawn. Looked fitter and better than ever, still unscarred, strong, the epitome of physical human perfection.

We were getting close to expanding the program, and I'd at last persuaded them to sign off on creating more like him. Partly, it was due to the incredible successes Adam had achieved in the field. But even more, it was a bad time in the war and they needed everything they could possibly use—human weapons included.

I told him the good news when he was in my lab getting blood drawn, and I could feel him stiffen. "We've refined the process," I reassured him. "The grafts will be smoother, allowing the surgeries and then recovery both to take less than half the time than before."

"Good," he said, but like that—without expression, ghostly.

"Yes, and the galvanizing catalyst is nearly perfect, thanks to the contributions from yourself and the others. We've tested it several times on human subjects, even without other procedures, and the results are spectacular. Once we've experimented further in the augmentations—"

Adam interrupted. "This is your greatest love, isn't it?"

It was, of course, as he knew well. We'd had conversations. He's intelligent and has an excellent scientific mind, if he chose to apply himself. He understood.

My greatest love…

That was why he burned it. At first, I thought it was to save other subjects from the procedures he had undergone. But it wasn't that—I'm not even sure he cared about them one way or another. It was because it was *my* life's work, the thing I loved above all else.

He broke into my lab some time during the night. Literally—he broke in. The wall was damaged in a way the fire wouldn't have caused: Adam must've gone straight through it. Then he mixed chemicals in such a way to allow himself time to escape unscathed and unsuspected before they went boom. Like I said, he was a smart kid, and he had training from the OSS.

I woke to fire alarms, then saw light from the fire and knew in that instant what had happened. Elizabeth and I arrived too late to do anything, but I rushed in anyway, hoping against hope to save some part of my research. It was too late. I stumbled out with just one box of files. Then, I spent the next three weeks in the hospital, recovering from third-degree burns.

No, you wouldn't know that by looking at me, would you? I recovered very well. Yes, indeed!

But I had lost everything. My life's work had been in that lab, and what remained that was not destroyed was mostly the collaborative efforts that belonged to the lab as a whole and to the government. What little I had saved was perhaps enough to set me on the right track, but years of work were lost.

Yes, that still stings. It hurt me deeply.

My dear Elizabeth was as convinced as I was that Adam was responsible, but by the time she made a formal complaint it was too late—he'd been deployed oversees. She made a ruckus, my Elizabeth. But she told me later that she could tell by the looks on their faces that it didn't matter one iota: Adam was more valuable to them than even me. They would never press charges against—or even investigate—one of their best assets. One augmented soldier in hand was better than a dozen possible ones in the lab.

It was their out.

They gave me facilities to continue research, of course. But it wasn't the same. What they really wanted was operatives they could use on clandestine missions—they had never shared my dream of perfecting humanity. Well—operatives they got. We got very good at honing and enhancing the extraordinary skills of those they found. Interesting work, at first. Even after I grew bored of it, Elizabeth persuaded me that these subtler ways of perfecting humanity might have as much value as the bold transformations I had dared dream of.

Perhaps I was willing to be persuaded, after seeing what Adam had become.

When the opportunity arose, I took a position in Washington where I could deepen my research into these techniques of enhancement...

I could talk for hours about that. You are not a scientist and have no interest in the breakthroughs I made, the setbacks, the hours I and my colleagues — including Elizabeth — poured into analyzing data, collating, testing. They were good times. Quiet. Productive. Peaceful.

What's that? Yes — you are right. Adam is the one I fear now — he is the one pursuing me. He will be my death.

There was no reason to think he chased me when he showed up in DC. The reasons he gave were good: escorting a VIP, doing some hush-hush reconnaissance work.

We encountered each other at a party. He smiled and said how good it was to see us again, but there was no denying the hatred in his eyes. No more was there any hiding the rancor we felt toward him, though we had no chance of confronting him about burning the lab. He made sure to never meet us privately.

Dr. Williams, one of my assistants and closest friends, was found stabbed to death in an alley a couple of nights after that party. They said he'd been mugged, but I knew...

We went to London soon after. Change of scenery — and they were doing some interesting work over there.

When Adam showed up in the back of a lecture hall where I was delivering a talk, there was no doubt in our minds that he had followed me there.

"We have to confront him — see what he wants, why he won't leave us alone," Elizabeth said, and I still remember her hand trembling on my arm.

It wasn't easy. I was afraid. But I agreed.

"Still the happy newlyweds," Adam said when we walked up to him. He was grinning, but it was ferocious, like a dog's snarl. "Every time I meet you, seems like you're happier than ever. How are you doing, Mrs. Franklin?"

"Why have you followed us?" Elizabeth demanded.

His grin grew even wider. But before anything could happen, a swell in the crowd separated us.

That night, my wife didn't come home. I searched, but... nothing.

The next morning...

Pass me another light, will you, son? Can't keep my hand steady.

Elizabeth was beaten and strangled and thrown into a broom closet. I should've stayed with her. I should have!

After that, I was sure they would do something about Adam. But it was the height of the war and things were bleak and no one listened to me. They needed him. They didn't have time for a fool grudge.

I kept seeing Adam over the next few weeks — across the street, at the other end of a crowded bus, sitting in the back of the church during the funeral. Sometimes I'd try to get close to him, but he always vanished. More often though, I didn't try... I was afraid. Terribly. The burning passion had returned to his eyes, but it was mixed with hatred.

It was useless waiting for him to be transferred or reassigned. For all I knew, he wasn't even part of the OSS anymore. So, I ran.

At first, I didn't admit I was running — merely going to Cambridge for a few weeks to consult a professor there, then to Aberdeen, then... But I was running, and Adam always followed.

I found myself in France soon after D-Day — trying to track down a subject to get a blood sample, or that was my excuse. One day, I came out of a half shelled-out hotel where I'd found shelter, and I found Adam just sitting there, on the rubble, in the drizzly rain, waiting for me.

"Well?" I said. Tired of running. Wanting to attack him but knowing it would be no use — he was too big, too strong, too... monstrous.

"Look what you've made of me," he said, just like he had all those years ago. He stretched out his hands so that I could see that he was still perfect under that battered uniform.

I said, "Only what you wanted."

Adam shrugged. "I was just a scrawny kid who wanted to be able to stand shoulder to shoulder with my fathers and not be ashamed. That's it. I didn't want... *this*."

"Too late now."

"Yes."

"Why not just accept it?" I asked.

"I have." Adam sounded practical, resigned. For the first time, I could see how he might look *normal*, in ordinary life — humorous, intelligent, good company even. But he went on: "You made me into a monster, so that's what I have become."

I stumbled back a step and he laughed at me.

"Are you still deluding yourself that you've made the uber-man, Dr. Franklin? You're more of a fool than I gave you credit for. You can't just cut up slabs of corpses and put them together again — I don't even know what parts are my own! You can't just break bones and tear nerves apart to sew them up with salvaged meat, then jolt it with an injection of God-knows what and call it a whole body!"

"You knew what you were getting into," I said, but he interrupted:

"You didn't tell me that you would sever my soul from my body, then tell me to live again in the shape of a dead monster! I died on that operating table, and you made me come back to un-life in this prison."

I was shaken, I must confess, but I shouted: "Why wreak vengeance on me? How was I to know? You have taken more from me than I took from you!"

"You took *everything* from me in exchange for this body that *you* wanted to create. And then you asked for more, and more, and more. I have no hope of freedom. My only purpose left is revenge."

"If you hate it so much, why don't you destroy yourself?"

"You don't think I haven't tried?" Adam half-smiled and looked out across the scarred landscape. "This is war. There is opportunity enough for those who seek death to meet it. Well, I met it. And it turned me down. I can't die, Dr. Franklin. That is what you have made of me."

He let me go after that, didn't pursue. Not then.

But afterwards, it was like a hunter going after prey. He means to kill me, now that he's taken everything from me. And I never see him now, except maybe a glimpse in the corner of my eye. Pushed me into the Seine in Paris, then shot at me in broad daylight on a busy street. Set fire to my room while I was sleeping. Grazed me and nearly shot my driver as I was on my way toward Strasburg. Blew up my car with a grenade when I reached it—I only just escaped. Actually shot me three days ago...

It's only a matter of time, you see. There's nothing I can do, no authority I can go to, no refuge where I can take sanctuary. Adam will find me and will kill me. I have nothing left—the only lasting thing I have accomplished is to earn his hatred.

He's finished.

Last stop, most passengers got off. Only one remaining is a man hunched up in the other corner under a blanket. It's dark. Dawn soon, if dawn ever comes.

Three whole minutes have passed. The old man remains silent.

Hell!

What do I say? If this story is true, then he's the maddest old bugger in existence, but pathetic. He presses his hand to his side, coughs. Blood on his handkerchief, but it's old. This cough was better.

I've seen wounds in that area before. Men don't usually walk away from them.

"You were shot three days ago, you say?"

Dr. Franklin smiles. Smirks is a better word. "I'm stronger than I look."

Another voice from somewhere: "I should've known. The doctor took some of his own medicine! So that's why you've been so hard to kill."

It's the man under the blanket. He's standing. One of the American GIs who was playing cards earlier. He's tall, young, fresh-faced like he hasn't seen a day of war. But his eyes —

Damnation! His eyes!

I must keep writing, or I'll go mad looking at those eyes. They're like the eyes of the dead after a battle.

Old man cringes into the corner: "Adam!"

I can't doubt the story now.

"I've always been close. Close enough to kill. Close enough to watch your agony, waiting for the blow to fall." Adam sits on a case near me. "It's been interesting hearing your side of the story, Dr. Franklin. Makes me realize how much of an unrepentant bastard you still are. You've been writing it down, haven't you? Well, I have little enough to add to the record. But as an impartial party, maybe you can judge: Was I wronged, being given little information about the cruel experiments to be exacted on me? How could I know that my hope of health and honorable service would be betrayed? Dr. Franklin has described himself as seeking only the betterment of humanity. But see what I am? Am I really an improvement? I am an abomination — a hodgepodge of parts passing as a man. My nerves are not my own, my blood is not my own, my bones are not my own! Sometimes, I can hear them, you know: The men whose shredded corpses are wrapped up in my skin. I hear them screaming. Guess that sounds crazy... Maybe I am crazy."

Dr. Franklin: "I'm sorry, Adam. I didn't know. How could we know? You were the first, and afterward we would have perfected the process, refined it. The next subjects would not have had to undergo the pain you experienced in the operation, and they would have been better, stronger, closer to perfection."

"Look at him." Adam lets out a breath as if he's achieved some victory. "Dr. Franklin still thinks I'm some kind of test subject in his lab — a failure that can be improved on. He still intends to do it, to make humanity better — by warping it beyond recognition. What does that make him?"

Silence.

He answers his own question: "Dangerous. Far more dangerous than I will ever be. And far crazier."

I agree. But I'm afraid of both these abominations, and now I'm trapped alone with them. How —

Adam looks at me like those dead eyes can read my thoughts. "I'm sorry for you, but this is it."

Dr. Franklin leans forward, almost rises. "Adam, please, have mercy. There might be something we can do to fix this — to cure you."

"There is no cure, no repair." Adam stands, takes a box from his pocket. Wires run from it toward both sides of the car. "This is vengeance, Dr. Franklin, for what you took from me: My life, everything I ever loved, every hope and dream, my death, my humanity. I am what you made me—a monster made by a monster."

It's a detonator. Damn! He's going to—

"The train crash will kill you if the explosion doesn't." Adam shrugs. "It might even kill me! If not, there's still fighting in Japan."

He's going to do it.

"Please, Adam, son!" Dr. Franklin says. "I'm sorry."

"So am I."

No—

From shorthand notes made in a damaged memoranda book found in wreckage of refugee train in eastern Europe. Owner not known.

The End

PATCHES
Michelle L. Levigne

'Na choked on a mouthful of cream cake and knew she was in trouble. A sparkling, pudgy bunny came bouncing down the forest path to the bank of the Snarl River. No bunny in his right mind would be caught within three leagues of the Snarl River.

Which meant this bunny had to be Fang, the wannabe vampire bunny, however greatly changed he was. While the pink and silver sparkles were confusing, he did bounce at crooked angles off every hard surface. And if that wasn't a strong enough clue, he had bloodstains on his enormous front teeth.

"Fang, what are you doing here?" Ambrose said.

'Na struggled to swallow the now-bitter mouthful of what had been a delicious apricot jam and cream cake the housekeeping breezes had made for Ambrose's birthday.

"Don't tell me the vampires threw you out again?" he added.

"They're probably jealous," 'Na muttered, and sniffed, afraid that some of the cream had gone up her nose.

"Those don't look like vampires," he said, struggling up from the picnic blanket and nearly stepping in the remains of their lunch. He gestured at a staggering, stumbling group that looked decidedly ragged and trailed a cloud of what seemed to be dust, visible even from a distance.

'Na wondered what sort of defensive magic they were carrying, because a herd of kispies should have detected them long before they approached the river and gone on the offensive. Kispies were generally offensive to begin with, but this was their swarming season, and the banks on both sides of the Snarl River were their home territory. They got rather touchy when it came to strangers intruding during swarming time. "Touchy" usually meant they made piranha look restrained and possessing good table manners.

Fortunately, they adored Lord Zared and Lady Ashlyn, who years ago had tracked down and defeated the source of an incredible stink that threatened to drive them out of their territory. That adoration extended to 'Na and now Ambrose, which made the banks of the Snarl River the perfect place to get some rare and precious privacy.

Fang hopped high and arrowed down between them, to land in the picnic basket with enough force to break several woven willow strips and squash the remains of their food. He squeaked and tugged the napkin over himself and shuddered hard enough to make the basket rock slightly.

"So, I take it he's having a problem with the rejuvenation spell?" Ambrose said, leaning down to look into the basket.

"I assume so." 'Na sighed. "Sorry, Fang. You don't want them to know you're here?"

The bunny's enormous ears stood up stiff and slapped backward three times before diving under the napkin again. An emphatic *no*.

She got to her feet and moved over to stand in front of the basket as the crowd of interlopers stomped closer. Ambrose stepped up next to her and discretely nudged the basket, so it slid under the branches of the pricklebush. Yet another reason to adore the man for his intelligence and supportive spirit.

"Is there something we can help you with?" Ambrose called, using that chill tone of voice that kept King Ruprick's courtiers from running roughshod over him and the servants who did the actual work of keeping the kingdom running smoothly. He leaned sideways toward 'Na and lowered his voice. "Other than hitting them with a spell to raise their intelligence? They need it, for daring to come banging through here and irritating the kispies just when they've settled down for their afternoon nap."

'Na muffled a snort and a snicker. Kispies didn't believe in naps. She devoutly hoped this unusual delay in vicious response meant they had retreated high above the trees, to give them a running start and double their speed when they finally made their attack.

"It be around here somewheres," the shortest man of the dusty group announced. He visibly consulted a tumbling, yellowish crystal hovering in the air above his gloved hand. He raised his head and speared 'Na with a glare from his beady eyes. "Where is it? You can't steal what's belonging to us."

"What do you think belongs to you?" She infused all the sharp-edged ice of the Beastly Beauty at her worst into her voice and gaze.

It startled her, for half a moment, that yes, she was becoming more like her mother every day.

"That fanged furry beasty is reeking of youth elixir, and we wants it, we needs it, and we is going to have it, no matter who we gotta hurt," the tallest and mangiest of the group announced, and punctuated his words with a stomp.

'Na's gorge rose as the tip of the man's nose and portions of his left ear fell off, crumbling to dust as they fell. The others in the motley crew were disintegrating as well -- faces and hair and clothes. That explained the dust.

"Yes, I can see you need it, but there is no youth elixir involved,"

Ambrose said. "The beasty is a vampire under a terrible curse, and if you make the mistake of touching it, you'll be infected with the same curse and twisted around the sundial until you don't know backward from forward."

"Say what?" The third man cleared his throat and hacked, nearly hitting the toe of 'Na's left boot.

The yelp of indignation caught in her throat when she saw the disintegrating left side of his face blur and then somehow un-disintegrate. There was some powerful magic at work here, and working at wonky wrong angles.

"Hey, boys -- look." The first man held out his hand with the hovering crystal. It pulsed a little faster as he stepped closer to 'Na. "It's her."

"What do you mean, it's her?" The fourth man had been silent up until this point. He turned his head so quickly to look at 'Na his entire scalp slid sideways, so his long, straggly hair half-covered his pockmarked face.

"How'd you turn the rabbit into the trollop?" He grinned so wide, the holes in his teeth were visible. A tooth fell out, hitting the edge of the picnic blanket with a sodden plop. Then it shattered. "That's powerful magic. Is it for sale?"

The shards of his tooth leaped back into his mouth, whole and white again.

'Na thought she might be sick.

"First of all, the Lady Belladonna is not a trollop," Ambrose seethed in arctic tones, stopping 'Na from saying Fang was a bunny, not a rabbit.

"And second," 'Na said, fighting laughter, "you're in enormous trouble." She yanked on his arm as she dropped to her knees and then flat on her face.

Ambrose, being the observant, clever young man she adored, followed her half a heartbeat later as the awakened, irritated, protective kispie swarm buzzed through the riverside clearing. Smaller than hummingbirds, they made charging elephant herds wince in terror. They had brought all their weaponry. Pikes and spears and swords and war axes so tiny had a tendency to be devastatingly sharp.

Shrieking, the Fang-hunters scattered. Some shattered. 'Na stared, slightly nauseated, as the fleeing men caught their scattering pieces and tried to slap them back into place in mid-flight. In moments, with the sparkling, hotly buzzing cloud of kispies driving them like an angry goatherd, the men fled back the way they had come.

"Well ..." Ambrose cautiously got up on his knees. "How long will that work?"

"Considering how rapidly they're disintegrating?" 'Na shuddered. "I have the awful feeling ... Fang, the regeneration spell went too far, didn't it?"

Fang popped his head out of the basket with the napkin draped over him like a maiden's veil. He let out a chirp and his ears bobbed rapidly in an agitated *yes*. 'Na sucked in a harsh breath. Just in the time he had been hiding, his fur looked fluffier, his cheeks were pudgier, and his massive front teeth had moved back together so the gap had vanished. The bloodstains of Fang's demented pride and joy had completely vanished. Meaning the original bite that nearly took his head off and started the gradual transformation into a vampire had been erased. Or was it more accurate to say it had been reversed?

"Picnic is over," Ambrose said with a sigh. Not at all a question. He had spent enough time with the residents of the enchanted castle, he didn't have to ask.

'Na bit her lip against remarking that even if they hadn't finished their meal, the picnic was over. Fang had devoured all the cream cake, the candied fruit, and the berry tartlets she had been saving for after she and Ambrose tried out the walking-on-water charms her father had given him for his birthday present this morning. In moments, they had shaken out the blanket and folded it to slide under Fang. They left the scraps of their lunch for the riverbank inhabitants and started up the trail back to the castle.

"Hello! Fancy meeting you out here," a familiar, jolly voice called through the shadows of the trail far ahead of them.

"No, please tell me he's not back with more trouble," 'Na murmured. "I thought Phibbia was reforming him."

"Unfortunately, I think she brought the trouble to Ruprick this time. She has some horrid, very distant relatives who should have stayed distant. They showed up at the castle maybe two days ago, proclaiming how delighted they were to know she had been released from the curse. The most oblivious one in the horde dared to ask which floor of the castle would be turned over to their family to live in. His Majesty was not … very welcoming. I imagine Ruprick and Phibbia are here to ask for help."

"Well, I supposed that shows her common sense is rubbing off on him," she admitted grudgingly.

Fang stirred and snorted and peered from under the napkin. His fur had taken on a hint of pink. 'Na wisely chose not to mention that. She knew she didn't have to warn Ambrose, but it would be better for all of them if Fang stayed out of sight. Ruprick was understandably terrified of Fang after their first encounter. He constantly teetered on the knife's edge of irritating and clumsily adorable, and he would say the wrong thing no matter how hard he tried to be clever and charming.

Unfortunately, Prince Ruprick carried a heavy burden of political training and excruciatingly good manners. He filled the journey to the castle by making all sorts of ridiculous small talk, asking how Ambrose and 'Na were doing, how much Ambrose was enjoying his fortnight of holiday for his birthday, how 'Na's parents were faring, if Zella was settling into her position as librarian and book tamer for the castle. On and on.

Fang grew irritated and restless. He growled, a little louder with each passing minute. And kept stiffening his ears, lifting the napkin until the gentle breeze threatened to lift it right off him and reveal his presence. 'Na said nothing to silence or calm him. She was honestly interested in seeing just how long it would take Ruprick to notice Fang — or wisely ignore him.

He really had gained some degree of courage and gallantry, since releasing Phibbia from her frog curse and marrying her.

"What is that?" Phibbia squeaked and pointed at the basket. "Is that a rabbit?"

Fang raised his head above the edge and glared at them. His growls grew louder with every heartbeat.

"No," Ruprick hurried to say. "That is a bunny, and don't irritate him. Please, darling, don't fear. He won't hurt you. It's me he has a grudge against. Quite justified, I must admit."

That confession brought a break in Fang's growls and he tipped his head to the side, studying Ruprick with rapid blinks, as if he wasn't quite sure what he looked at.

Ruprick reached in his belt pouch and brought out a small cloth bag. "Hello, Fang. I thought you might enjoy these." He handed the pouch to Ambrose and stepped back quickly, out of jumping range. "A new confection. Chewy, with a liquid center, and very red. It's rather fun, actually, to suck the juice out," he added with a forced chuckle.

'Na nearly choked as Fang purred and ducked back under the napkin, clutching the bag Ambrose handed him. Well, maybe Ruprick had grown a great deal smarter than she had given him credit for. Loud sucking noises emerged from under the napkin.

~~~~~

Two hours later, Lady Ashlyn shook her head. She stepped back from the diagnosis and isolation ring. Braided from iron, silver and gold, it surrounded Fang, lying on a table in the magical artifacts storage and nullification room. A single tear dripped from Fang's left eye. He curled up tighter around himself, closed his eyes, and hid his face with his ears.

"That's the best we can do for him," Lord Zared said. "The ring will halt the spell until we can find something to cancel it permanently." A snort escaped him. and he cocked an eyebrow at Ambrose, who had settled the visitors and joined them half an hour into the examination and discussion. "Does your family line have any seers?"

"Sir?" Ambrose took a step back. "May I ask why?"

"Your comment to those idiots about wrapping around the sundial is
~~~~~

part of the answer. We need to anchor Fang to time again, and get him moving forward at a normal pace. To do that, we need an expert in time-related magic, to convince the body to return to its former state."

"How did we bungle the regeneration spell so badly?" 'Na fought down a recurring wave of nauseated guilt at the thought that she had done this to Fang. Not just the possibility that he would continue reversing until he became a bunny kit and then vanish, but making him the object of greedy and confused spell hunters like those disintegrating idiots.

"We didn't." Ashlyn narrowed her eyes at Fang, who flinched slightly even though his eyes were closed and he couldn't see her expression. That was a remnant of the bond they had had in their younger days. She gestured for the other three to follow her. "However, because you read the spells over him, to initiate the cure ... well, thanks to some meddling from inside the spell, and a know-it-all bunny who refuses to follow instructions, you're tangled with the problem. That's why the scrying crystal pointed at you and those idiots thought you were Fang hiding under a transformation spell. The rings should do their job to not only halt his changes but sever the connection between you two."

While she spoke, the four of them left the corner of the room, an offshoot of the healing magic books wing of the library, where Fang apparently would have to stay until they found his cure. She led the way out of the maze of shelves and chests and cages. The miasma of enchantments subtly struggling for dominance cleared when they stepped out into the hall. Zared pulled hard on the iron ring until the heavy oak and iron-bound door thudded ponderously shut.

"Fang was overzealous, as usual. The scrying glass showed me glimpses of him eating several youth charms before and after we worked those decrepitude spells backward. After we specifically told him to fast beforehand, and then sit still and let the magic settle in and solidify once we did our work. Fang always did think he knew better." Ashlyn sighed.

"We wouldn't be together, darling, if he wasn't a headstrong idiot, determined to do things his own way and go the extra league or two," Zared said, wrapping an arm around her waist.

"True." She reached out to cup 'Na's cheek. "So, don't blame yourself a moment longer, dearest. That was clever thinking. You're quite the disenchanter and riddle solver, and you make us proud. You and Ambrose will be a formidable team in your own right, after some seasoning."

"If we live that long," 'Na muttered.

The next step was to consult Zella, as the full-time castle librarian, in charge of updating all the newest magical happenings and developments. That was handled far more easily than 'Na had managed when she was solely in charge of the library. Now that Zella's mirror, Primp had joined forces with Eyesallova, the enchanted castle's resident magic mirror, they missed out on far fewer incidents and caught more useful, juicy gossip. The mirrors shared monitoring the magic mirror network, so there was far less noise to filter out, and they could take breaks to socialize. Working together, they kept Zella and 'Na updated, and the two childhood friends shared recording and cross-referencing the information they gathered. The books were happier and better behaved with two librarians to look after them. They also loved having extra information inserted into their pages. 'Na and Zella agreed that some of the books prided themselves on being plump and needing extension strips added to their binding, to hold all the new pages.

When Ambrose and 'Na went in search of Zella, they found her hauling books away from a shoulder-high pile in front of the double main library doors. She turned to look at them, shrugged, and bent for another armful. 'Na paused and listened, and sure enough, heard a rumbling sort of unhappy snuffling coming from the other side of the door.

"Smedley?" Ambrose said, pitching his voice to a whisper.

Zella rolled her eyes. She opened her mouth to respond, then her smile shattered into a scowl. "No, you don't!" She stomped over to an eye-level shelf where the books were sidling to the front edge, teetering and about to dive off. "When are you dust-catchers going to learn to trust me? When I say no dragons allowed in the library, I mean no dragons. I will not allow him past the doors. Every time you jump off the shelves, you're weakening your bindings. Do you really enjoy having me slather you with glue and stick needles into you to put you back together?"

Rasping, the books moved to the back of the shelf.

'Na and Ambrose helped Zella herd the other books back to their shelves. She explained the newest quest, to help Fang reverse his increasing youthfulness. Zella's hair twitched several times, reacting to the discussion. In the three months since she chopped it off to foil Prince Rumpton's evil magical real estate scheme, it had grown to a mass of reddish gold-streaked tight curls extending out from her head to elbow length. In all directions. Some curls obligingly tightened to hold pens and bookmarks, styluses, and small pads of paper, so she didn't try to restrain any of them. She frowned in thought, her gaze distant, as she reshelved books and argued with several that didn't want to be put back next to their assigned neighbors. Several longer strands of hair twined together into thick coils that sometimes snapped out at particularly recalcitrant books.

"I'm positive Eyesallova mentioned something about a right-to-copy dispute, centered on that hermit ..." Zella murmured. "Now what was his name? The one who is making strides in copying physical features as well as qualities onto people and objects. The intent was to cut down on heroes having their heroic aspects magically stolen outright, while allowing for duplication and multiplication of their strengths in times of crisis."

"You don't mean Zerocs, do you?" Ambrose paused with two thick tomes raised to slide onto a shelf. "That's a name I've been hearing too much lately, back at the palace."

"Don't tell me." She dusted her hands on her tunic and turned to face him and 'Na. "King Ruprick is making another attempt at setting up a wizarding collegium, and he's having temper tantrums when no one accepts his invitations?"

"Oh, several accepted, but then they've tacked on all sorts of conditions and expectations that will bankrupt the kingdom." He surprised 'Na by grinning. "One benefit of him screaming until he goes hoarse is he can't talk for two days afterward. He's too vain to admit he can't write more than his name, so he spends a great deal of time alone when that happens. Can't order people about if he can't communicate, can he? His temper is ten times worse when he regains his voice, and he has a tendency to take tripled retribution on people who irritated him while he was silent. A lot of the troublemakers in the Court have been taking long visits to their country estates, to stay off his naughty list, so it's much nicer at the palace nowadays."

"However?" 'Na prompted.

"Zerocs wants an entire squadron of advocates working for him, tracking down everyone who has been appropriating his copying spell without permission or paying user fees, and fighting off everyone who has been coming up with difficulties, such as disfigurement and untimely fading of the spells they claim they paid exorbitant fees to use, but those fees never reached Zerocs. Someone trying to win his favor created a curse on anyone who doesn't pay the fee, so the spell warps, diluted into low quality, and fades out quickly and unevenly. Plus, there are people who copy from the copy they made, thinking the first fee protects them from the curse, which just means the blurring and warping happens even more quickly. It can be quite messy, and of course, everyone wants to blame Zerocs and make him fix the problems they created, instead of admitting they stole and broke the rules."

"So explain to me how a wizard who is specializing in copying spells can deal with the time-anchoring problem to heal Fang?"

"Have you heard the song about the wizard of space and time?" he said. "It was written about him, maybe ... twenty years ago."

"Meaning he's good advertising for his own product." She nodded and felt a little curl of relief on Fang's behalf. Not that the stubborn idiot deserved her sympathy right now.

"It does sound like he's the wizard we need, if we're going to return Fang to his former state. If he's near a mirror network, we can save time on traveling ..." Zella's smile fell off hard enough 'Na almost heard the crash. "However … problem."

"No one knows where he's hiding right now?" 'Na guessed. Then another thought hit her, so she stumbled backward a step. "Those idiots out in the forest."

"Which ones now?" Zella said. "There are so many wandering the enchanted forest, we should really institute a spell to slap nametags on all of them and keep a logbook that automatically updates. Or maybe get one of Primp's freelance friends to come work for us just to monitor the forest."

"The ones who were hunting Fang, thinking he had a fountain of youth spell. What better way to fix a disintegrating spell than reverse the decay process? If they're cheap enough to try to patch the good parts of other people onto themselves, instead of paying to have maji-cosmetic surgery, then they're foolishly cheap enough to pay spell bandits instead of the creator and owner of the original spell."

"And now they're paying for it." Ambrose shuddered. "I'm not surprised Zerocs has become a hermit, with all the trouble relating to his spell, and people trying to punish him for the trouble they brought on themselves by cheating."

The next step was to consult Eyesallova and Primp and start the search for gossip that would lead them to Zerocs's hiding place.

"Did you say Zerocs?" Primp broke in, as soon as 'Na said the name.

"Yes. What have you heard?" Ambrose said.

"The man is a lunatic when it comes to cooking potions. I relay orders for five or six bottles from Granny Pepper every three days. Whenever she comes up with a new recipe, he orders four bottles, without taking advantage of the free samples." Primp's surface spun with green-purple swirls.

"Where are you having them delivered?"

"That's the sticking point. Every moon, a different drop-off point." She sniggered. "He's paranoid about being followed. From what our delivery people have said, he's got no reason to be worried."

"Meaning?" Zella said.

"Some bizarre patchwork monster protects him. Depending on who's watching, and how close they get, if they see it in twilight or moonlight, it has five heads and fifty eyes and ten arms and twenty legs and five tails, and it's covered in bolts. Lightning bolts and metal bolts like what holds together that metal bridge monstrosity over Bottomless Chasm."

"That's … interesting." 'Na made up her mind to ask her parents to come with them on this quest. She wasn't ashamed to admit they might be in over their heads this time.

Unfortunately, when she went in search of her parents, Ashlyn and

Zared were in the courtyard, checking their bags before mounting their horses to ride out with Ruprick and Phibbia. A simple scrying spell had revealed several threads of magic trying to wrap around the new bride and sink roots in her. Zared had initiated a tracking spell and his tattletale map spell drew multiple lines across several kingdoms, revealing that Phibbia's relatives had been driven out of their homes when the frog spell on her broke. That was magical justice, because they had initiated the spell in a scheme to take her father's throne. When the spell broke, it backlashed all of them.

This was the perfect opportunity to put King Ruprick even more firmly in the debt of the lord and lady of the enchanted castle and force him into long-term good manners. They would bring his unwanted guests to justice, publicly humiliating them, and free Ruprick from the curse of noxious in-laws, all at the same time. The task would take several days and needed to be handled immediately. The threads of magic Ashlyn had removed from Phibbia revealed the in-laws were in the process of using their connection with her, and her freshly made bonds with Prince Ruprick, to sink roots into the kingdom, likely intending to take it over. Perhaps even turning Ruprick, father and son, into frogs.

"Better the pompous boor we know than the ones we don't," Zared said. "No offense, Ruprick."

"None taken. I quite agree." Ruprick chuckled. He sounded even less brainless than usual. Love seemed to have worked some favorable magic on him. 'Na was impressed.

Half an hour after Zared and Ashlyn rode into the forest with Ruprick and Phibbia, the disintegrating idiots came trotting up the path to the castle gate, following that irritating yellow crystal. The housekeeping breezes turned into miniature twisters, picking up pebbles and leaves and branches from the decorative bushes, and scoured the intruders. They shouted and flung what looked like sand into the air. It flared sickly shades of orange and green and formed a defensive dome, allowing them to move forward. After only ten steps, the dome crumpled like wet, wrinkled parchment.

Zella, Ambrose and 'Na were in the mirror room. Eyesallova showed them what happened outside the castle while Primp worked on tracking down the destination of the next order for Zerocs.

"That's disintegrating magic," the mirror commented, and tsked. "It's faded, and fading more every time they use it."

"Bad copies," Zella said. "Maybe copies of copies. That's what they get for cheating."

Over the next hour, they watched as the intruders tried to break down the main gate of the castle. The four spells they threw at it malfunctioned just as badly as the shielding spell. The housekeeping breezes continued pelting them, with pebbles and dead plants and water and toothy, carnivorous fish from the moat. One spell caused carpets of flowers to sprout in the wood of the gates and root in the stones of the archway. In a few heartbeats, those flowers faded and died and disintegrated. Much like the noses and fingers and hair and chins and biceps of the intruders.

"This is embarrassing, and a little nauseating," 'Na commented, after the attackers had to stop for the fifth time to repair their own bodies.

"We need to find a way to get that metal chest away from them," Eyesallova said. "They're bringing the spell copies out of it. Have you noticed that flash of light, just when they slide the lid sideways and take out the next replacement?"

"I could try shooting a pike at them to pierce the chest, with a rope attached. Like the harpoons used to capture sea monsters," Ambrose said. "Just haul it to us."

A gulping, snuffling sound came from the doorway of the chamber. 'Na looked up to see Smedley the dragon, wide-eyed and eager. His face was all she could see, and he had to stretch his neck likely to the point of pain to get his head to the doorway. Her childhood friend had grown enormously since that accident in the library that had necessitated him leaving the castle. He couldn't fit through the narrower hallways of the castle. Fortunately, he was a very serpentine breed of dragon, with a neck nearly ten cubits long, and a tail twice that. However, the barrel of his chest, where the fire-breathing ability originated, was now as wide as a blacksmith's shop.

"Oh, I don't know if that would be wise," Eyesallova said. "'Na, do stop him before he makes a mess." She let out a sigh as Smedley's blue and green-scaled face vanished from the door.

"What is he going to do?" 'Na needed to find that browband made of Smedley's childhood scales, that allowed her to understand what he was saying. She had put it away somewhere when her dragon friend left. The castle had grown so much in the intervening years she wasn't sure what room held the chest where she had left it.

"Steal the chest, probably." Ambrose ran out of the room, in pursuit.

"Smedley means well, dear," Eyesallova said. "He's just not housebroken anymore."

"More like breaking the castle," Primp said. "The question is, do those enormous wings of his work?"

"I don't really know. Why?" 'Na said.

"Traveling by horseback won't get you to the drop-off place in time to catch whoever or whatever is picking up Zerocs's order."

"We'll take a shortcut through the corridor dimensions." She started to shrug, then froze as she understood. "You want us to ride Smedley?"

"Ride Smedley?" Ambrose blurted as he returned to the mirror room. "Why? Where?"

"More important, did you stop him?"

"For now. I told him you had a nasty trick you wanted to play on the village idiots." He grinned. "Please tell me that will include some of the nobles? Maybe fly by some of their castles on our way back?"

"Oh, you two are perfect for each other," Eyesallova muttered. She and Primp shared a few chiming giggles.

"That would work out," Primp added. "On the way back. The drop-off place for Zerocs's next order is in the Stonenfrahnk Forest."

"Of course. Where else would it be?" 'Na said.

"What's Stonenfrahnk?" Ambrose said. "I've never heard of it."

"It's essentially a no-magic zone imposed by the Sylvan faeries."

"That should be ... comforting?"

"They aren't very good about following or enforcing their own rules."

"Ah. Sounds like a good number of the nobility I've had the misfortune to meet."

'Na had to resist the urge to fling her arms around him and give him a kiss to show him just how glad she was he was here. She grinned the next moment as she came up with a nasty trick, just as Ambrose had a promised Smedley.

Actually, it was a nasty trick she had wanted to play for some time, most often on Fang. A quick visit to the storage room for useful magical items produced the bag of accommodation. Then they retrieved Fang from the protective magical rings that halted the over-active rejuvenation spells. That was going to be the tricky part. 'Na explained what she wanted to do, and Fang's very necessary part as bait. For a few seconds, she feared the utterly too-adorable bundle of sparkly pink and white chubbiness had lost his hyper-vicious attitude. He just blinked at her with big, liquid eyes. Then that manic spark filled them and Fang bounced up and down in eagerness.

She gave the bag of accommodation to Ambrose, because he could run faster than her, while she ran after him clutching Fang, with a spell-slowing silver and iron net wrapped around him. Ambrose got to the outer garden gate before her and set up the bag, stretching it wide and anchoring it with ropes to the frame of the gates, which opened outward. He left one side open, for 'Na to reach in and toss the cuddly armful of Fang into the mouth of the bag, which was now wide and tall enough for all four of the attackers to walk into.

That was kind of the plan.

Fang saluted her with wide sweeps of his ears, which disconcertingly gave off pink and blue and gold sparks. 'Na darted back and fastened the side of the bag to the gate. Ambrose climbed up and unbarred the gate, and gave one side a good, hard kick so it swung wide open.

As hoped, that wretched yellow gem led the four disintegrating idiots straight to the gate, with Fang sitting and sparkling faintly in the shadows of the wide open maw of the bag of accommodation. With yelps of triumph, the four men ran without a second of hesitation for common sense, right into the bag. Ambrose leaped down, pulling on the rope of the drawstring, closing the bag. It shrank down to normal size rapidly enough that none of the prisoners inside had time to realize they were suspended in time and trapped.

Fang was also suspended, his dangerous rejuvenation halted, and that was more important to 'Na than keeping those four idiots from ravaging the outside of the castle. She and Ambrose exchanged triumphant grins as the housekeeping breezes swirled around them, the air heavy with the celebratory scents of chocolate and raspberries, apricots and honeysuckle.

The celebration only lasted a few moments. The housekeeping breezes had to repair all the damage they had done to the landscaping in their efforts to protect the castle and irritate the attackers. Ambrose had a sparkle in his eyes that made 'Na very hopeful he was going to indulge in a celebratory kiss.

Then a roar echoed across the moat, and something massive broke through the trees on the far side of the western meadow where enchanted castle met enchanted forest. Lightning flashed, without a cloud in the sky. Then a few heartbeats later, thunder rumbled across the landscape. Trees shuddered and swayed, then fell to the right and left as something emerged from the shadows between them. More lightning danced across the shape.

"What is that?" Ambrose murmured.

"I've never seen anything like it." 'Na shrugged. "What I can see of it. The lightning bolts keep getting in the way." A queasy sensation, partially from memory, made her pause and swallow hard. "Do you see … six heads? And at least four pairs of arms? And a dozen legs?" She tried to smile when Ambrose nodded. "Good, then I'm not hallucinating."

"You check the library. I'll go ask the mirrors."

"Good idea."

Holding hands, they ran through the garden to the nearest door inside, which an obliging breeze swung open for them. Smedley roared from the roof of the castle, where he had gone to wait. He sounded rather plaintive. He hadn't had his chance to play a nasty trick yet.

In the main hallway, they split up, she to the library to find Zella, and he up the stairs to the sun room and the two magic mirrors. She shouted to the librarian and Zella stumbled out to meet her, clutching four newer books to her chest and looking panicked. The books seemed to be struggling to fling themselves open, and pages and bindings crackled.

"They're trying to come apart," Zella gasped, nearly losing the last word as the cover of one book punched her low in her ribs. "These are copied books. I don't understand."

"What do you—" 'Na stumbled two steps, then hurried to follow her friend back into the library, where some of the protective magic visibly calmed the struggles of the books. "Copied, as in Zerocs's spell? So the curse on the copying spell thieves is trying to take them apart?"

"They're legitimately made, with a long-term spell use license. Something is pulling at them, trying to take them apart, pulling at any of the books that were copied in one way or another." She dropped the books into a cage of thread-thin wires of silver and iron and gold that several housekeeping breezes were still assembling. Zella took a deep breath and braced herself on the cage. "What just happened out there, that they're reacting to?"

"Something is approaching the castle. Like I've never seen before … except when that stupid birthday curse hit me." She winced a little at the confession, but at least she didn't have to explain further. Zella knew what had happened.

"Obviously tied into the copying curse …" Frowning, she turned and hurried into the deeper recesses of the library, where the shelves reached to the vaulted ceiling and obliging breezes were needed to float up to access them.

One lifted her to a corner shelf up at the ceiling. She asked 'Na to describe what she saw as she searched the dark and dusty shelves, stopping to apologize to the sleeping books. A number of books shuddered and tried to leap off the shelves when 'Na described the streaks of lightning writhing around the creature's multiple heads and arms and legs.

"You have got to see this," Ambrose announced, his voice strained with effort, as he staggered into the aisle between the shelves. He carried Primp on his back. Sweat ran down his face and stained his shirt. The smaller magic mirror was as tall as him, wider than his torso, the layers of enspelled glass and silver backing as thick as his arm. He put Primp down, to lean against one tall bookshelf.

The image showed the oncoming creature now halfway across the meadow, crossing with a stomping, rocking sort of gait. It had four stiff sets of legs. Horse, bull, elephant, and dog legs. Three sets of legs appeared to have modified horseshoes on them, to make them the same length. They were all attached to what looked like the frame of a massive rocking horse, like a giant child would ride. In the midst of six heads, the rocking horse stared straight ahead with glass eyes and gaudy paint and a yarn mane.

The other heads were dragon, a lion, a snake, an eagle, and two dogs that snarled and foamed at the mouth. Multiple sets of arms ranged down the sides of the creature, clawing and swiping at the air, and interfering with three different sets of wings. A snake's tail writhed at the back, tangling with the yarn tail of the rocking horse and the swinging snap of a scorpion's tail.

Each head or other appendage attached to the gaudily painted rocking horse body with two silver bolts on each that shot off tiny flares of lightning. Jagged silver lines like silver threads in a thick blanket stitch filled the gap between attachment and wooden body. Every time those individual lightning flares met up, they merged into a thick bolt that flashed silver-white bright, and let out a crack of thunder.

The dog heads stretched forward on their long necks, noses twitching, sniffing the breeze. 'Na shuddered, knowing in her gut they were following the scent of those four idiots ... right to the bag of accommodation, which she and Ambrose had left lying in the open garden gates. She looked at him.

"We need to get that bag out of there," Ambrose said, before she could speak.

Definitely, Ambrose had seers in his bloodline, because he was reading her thoughts.

"That thing has to be tied to whatever is attacking the copies and whatever magic created the copies," Zella said. "What I don't understand is how it's affecting all the spells, made by different enchanters. It shouldn't be able to do that."

"It's a patchwork monster, all different pieces, maybe different pieces of spells, as well as different creatures?" 'Na said, thinking aloud.

"I don't know much about magic. Yet," Ambrose hurried to add, with a strained grin, when both 'Na and Zella let out a simultaneous muffled "ha!" "But doesn't that violate the spell right of copying law or curse or whatever?"

"It could be a multiple-class magic users' action," Primp offered. "There's been some muttering about rising frustration over violating the right to copy lots of other major classes of spells. Wait while I consult Eyesallova. She's more widely versed in such things." The images remained on her surface, but they grew hazy as she switched to private communication with the other magic mirror.

"We might not have that much time to wait," 'Na muttered. The patchwork monster was nearly to the moat, and she imagined those multiple sets of patched-in wings would work just fine to fly over. Its gait was stiff and slow, but it didn't need a running start, did it?

"Smedley," Ambrose said. Then without explaining, he grinned and ran out of the library.

"What's he doing?" Zella flipped open one of the books she had brought from those dark, upper shelves, and ran her finger down the index, searching.

"Getting the bag out of Patches' reach, I hope." 'Na hated feeling useless. Even more, she hated the feeling that she knew the answer, a solution for the problem, but it coyly stayed just around the corner in her mind and wouldn't come out to play.

"Patches?" She paused but never looked up from the page. "The monster. Makes sense."

"At least something does. I don't know how, but I know it's after those idiots in the bag —Hah!" She nearly slammed her fists on the table as the answer stepped out into the light where she could see it. That might knock a few books off the table. Not a smart thing to do in a library full of magical books. "Primp, can you contact Zerocs directly? Lie if you have to, tell him it has to do with his next shipment, tell him there's a problem with delivery."

"What kind of problem? It'll have to be pretty severe to make him break his silence," the magic mirror responded.

"Severe enough that if he doesn't call off Patches, Granny Pepper will take him off her customer list."

"Oooh, nasty!" The mirror chuckled. "I'm proud of you."

Then the mirror's surface grew cloudy enough the patchwork monster was little more than a writhing lump of darkness shot with silver flashes of lightning. 'Na held her breath as it leaped and glided over a dark streak in the ground that had to be the moat. Overhead, Smedley roared, the sound underscored by a crackling like coach-sized bellows blew on a bed of coals as big as the banqueting table in the great hall.

"There's nothing I can do here," Zella said, "and I really want to see what happens next."

'Na didn't even try to pretend she felt otherwise. Grinning, she turned and ran, heading for the closest balcony looking out over the gardens. Zella was right behind her. In less than two minutes, 'Na skidded through the door and caught herself before she toppled over the railing.

Smedley and Patches dove for the twitching bag of accommodation, which lay just inside the garden gates. They hit at the same time, one coming from the ground, the other from the air, and the stone and wood of the garden gates vanished in a mushroom-shaped, expanding cloud of splinters and grit.

"Sorry," Ambrose called from the far end of the castle rooftop.

'Na made a mental note to tell him later that her mother hated that gate. It was one of the few remaining original outer features of the castle. She wasn't sure why her mother hated that gate but knew Lady Ashlyn would laugh when she returned and saw it demolished.

"That's ... quite impressive." Zella tipped her head back to take in the growing cloud, and the two creatures swinging around each other in the air overhead. The pivot point was the bag of accommodation. Patches had caught it in the lion's mouth, while Smedley had the talons of one foot hooked through the drawstring. Their wings flapped and stuttered, sending gusts of wind down on the castle.

"If only there was a way to unmake all those spells holding Patches together," 'Na mused, thinking aloud. "Those spells attaching the extra pieces and parts certainly look like sewing. With enspelled silver thread. Any way to ... I don't know, make the silver corrode, or find the catch stitch and make it all unravel?"

"I don't think we have enough time to figure out how. Just how sturdy is that bag?"

"My parents stored a dozen troublesome ogres in it for about two moons, back when I was six or seven. Other than having to air it out and leave it propped open with a couple dozen scented candles ... no damage that they could detect."

"Too bad we couldn't get the bag open from so far away and stuff both of them inside."

"Yes, but the village idiots and Fang are already inside. There would be more than enough room, but it really isn't fair to Fang and Smedley."

The pocket mirror 'Na kept in her belt pouch flashed, meaning one of the magic mirrors needed to speak with her. She groaned and headed back into the castle.

The groan quickly became a sigh of relief: Zerocs had broken his silence.

At least, he was willing to talk until Zella joined them in the room. He paled and his eyes went glassy. His mouth moved several times, letting out a warped, gargled sort of vowel sound.

"Excuse me?" 'Na said. "Primp, has that idiot Rumpton figured out how to mess with the mirror network again?"

"It's not the connection." The mirror's shimmering tone meant she tried hard not to laugh. "I think we just found the bargaining chip in dealing with the mad genius."

"Mad" meant both insane and furious, it turned out. The story they unraveled more than a moon later was simple, and slightly embarrassing. Zerocs was madly in love with Granny Pepper's previously unnamed assistant. He lacked the courage to speak to her beyond placing his orders. He ordered so often as an excuse to talk to Zella. When she vanished and the mirror network took over handling orders, he took his frustration out on the counterfeits and thieves using his copying spell. He assembled Patches to hunt down anyone who used a stolen or counterfeited copying spell.

As soon as 'Na understood what Primp was inferring, she pulled Zella out of the pickup range of the mirror. Zerocs, who was admittedly much better looking than a tower-bound spellcasting genius had any right to be, let out a yelp and reached forward as if he would fling himself through his side of the magic mirror.

"She'll come back once you handle the problem with your monster that's fighting with my dragon," 'Na said. "How do you unravel all that magic stitchery and take apart your patchwork monster?"

"But—but—but—"

"We've already captured the four idiots who were using your copy spell and harassing my vampire bunny."

"Your what?" More awareness touched Zerocs's eyes, driving away some of the panic. He shook his head.

"I'll explain later. The spell?"

By that time, Ambrose had caught up with them. That was a good thing because Zerocs had to say the spell himself where Patches could hear, so the three needed to take Primp out to the balcony. Patches and Smedley were still spinning around each other and starting to turn an interesting shade of pea soup green. Zerocs spent the staggering trip down the halls and up the stairs staring beseechingly at Zella, who blushed and kept closing her eyes at the wrong time—it made walking tricky at best.

They propped Primp against a bench on the long balcony, so her surface looked up at the sky and captured the struggling beasts. Then Zerocs got to work, muttering and mumbling and twisting his fingers into knots. Every few sentences, he burst out with, "Uhndoo!" Alternating with something that sounded like, "Coon troll Zee!" At each shouted command, a set of silver bolts popped out, the stitching evaporated in a shower of sparks, and a copied piece of anatomy fell off Patches. It crumbled into dust that vanished into thin air a heartbeat later.

Zerocs had the sense not to remove Patches' wings until near the end of the struggle. That would have made things extremely awkward, otherwise. As it was, the patchwork monster let out a pathetic whining sort of roar, let go of the bag of accommodation, and fluttered awkwardly to the ground. Smedley hovered for a few weary beats of his wings, then dropped the bag on the balcony at 'Na's feet and came in for a bumpy landing. He kept his gaze fastened on Patches, and made it very clear he still meant business, with tiny spurts of flame from his nostrils every third or fourth breath.

After that, Zerocs tangled his fingers and spoke faster, and soon the only thing that remained of Patches was the wooden rocking horse.

"Let's deal with the village idiots right away," 'Na said, and gestured at the bag of accommodation. Ambrose grinned and darted forward with her, to each grab a corner with one hand and the end of the drawstring with the other. They pulled the bag open and dumped it onto the balcony, shaking hard. The four disintegrating attackers tumbled out at the foot of the mirror with yelps and snarls and whimpers.

Zerocs had been gazing somewhat sappily into the eyes of Zella, who reciprocated, blushing. Jolted out of his apparently happy daze, he glared down at the foursome, who looked much the worse for wear. More mumbled words, ending with a roared, "Uhndoo!" and the crumbling bits and pieces of the foursome vanished. They became solid again, and the copied features went back to what 'Na supposed were their original state: twisted, oversized or scrawny in all the wrong places, warty, with thick hairs growing out of noses and ears and chins.

"We be back the way we was!" their spokesman wailed.

As one person, they turned on Fang, who was now the size of two handfuls of sparkly pink, lavender, and white fur. 'Na quite understood why he preferred being at least part vampire. She thought she might grow nauseous in another moment with the overload of treacly sweetness emanating from him.

"This weren't what we was wanting!" the leader shouted and leaped at Fang, hands curled into visibly arthritic claws. Ambrose threw himself down, blocking their path, while 'Na leaped in and snatched up Fang. He scrambled up onto her shoulder and hid under the cover of her half-dismantled braids.

Zerocs spat out a stream of rapid-fire words that had 'Na's mouth aching in sympathy. Octopus arms wreathed in lightning appeared from slits in the air. Silver bolts appeared, attaching the new appendages to the rocking horse. It rocked back and forth as lightning sewed the arms to its body. Lightning flashed from its nostrils and eyes. The octopus arms writhed and curled, whipping around for a few heartbeats before the re-born Patches rocked forward in a huge, vicious leap. The four village idiots caught on too late, screamed, and tried to run. They only managed two steps before Patches landed on them. The octopus arms entangled them. One shrieked something semi-coherent about being allergic to seafood before the long, writhing, orange and pea-green tentacles wrapped around their mouths and torsos. Zerocs shouted more incoherent words. Patches rocked away, through the rubble of the gates and out of sight.

"Where are you taking them?" Ambrose asked.

"I have a seeking spell already at work, to take me to the counterfeiter who's been illegally selling people mangled copies of my copying spell." Zerocs sighed as he turned and his gaze caught with Zella's again. The two of them drifted a step closer, eyes getting wide and dreamy, mouths melting into sappy smiles. Until the surface of Primp stopped them.

For a moment, 'Na was alarmed for Zella's sake. Had some enemy enchanter attacked while they were distracted, hitting her with a love potion, heavy on treacle?

No, she considered Zella one of the most sensible and magic-resistant people she knew, so … was this real? She was all for infatuation and the promise of forever-after like her parents had. At least, she believed so. 'Na sent up a quick, desperate prayer that she didn't look quite so sappy and low on breathable air when she was dreaming about Ambrose.

"You're welcome to come visit," she hurried to say. Mostly to stop Zella from trying to walk through the surface of the mirror again. "We have the most extensive magical library for several kingdoms in all directions, and Zella is our head librarian. I'm sure she'd love to share it with you."

The wide-eyed look of gratitude Zella sent her made her feel even more guilty about her thoughts the last few moments.

"I … I can come visit? After …?" Zerocs gestured at the destruction littering the garden.

"If you bring Patches with you, with extra heads for reading and extra arms to help with repairing and shelving books, we'll consider it even. Yes?" Ambrose added, looking back and forth between 'Na and Zella.

Zerocs blushed bright red and gave off a few silver sparks when both young women agreed enthusiastically.

Zella sighed, with stars in her eyes, when Zerocs apologized profusely, his tongue tangling a few times, and vanished from the mirror.

"Sorry, Fang," 'Na said, and plucked the trembling, squeaking bundle of candy-scented bunny fur from under her hair. "It's back into the bag until we figure out how to age you forward again." She tossed him into the bag of accommodation and yanked the drawstrings closed.

Funny, but for all the times she had wanted to do that to him, it didn't feel even a tenth as satisfying as she had hoped. Sighing, she joined Ambrose at the balcony railing and looked around the ruins of the garden. Zella's gaze was on a spot far in the distance.

"How soon do you think they'll get here?" Zella said

"Not soon enough to help with the repairs." 'Na snorted. "It's going to be interesting explaining this one to my parents." She hooked her arm through Ambrose's and leaned her head on his shoulder. "I'm sorry. This wasn't exactly what we had planned for your birthday."

"Considering what Ruprick and I did on your birthday?" He grinned. "I think we're even. And look on the bright side. This time we didn't even have to leave the castle."

The End

NOT MY FAULT
C.S. Wachter

The pre-dawn darkness fled as a smudge of light appeared between the hills beyond the lake. The sky that had been inky now shown a pearlescent blue. The birds' musical greetings of the new day filled the air. A song of nature. A song of peace. Where had my peace gone? I sat unmoving, numb, the coffee in front of me cold in the chilly October air.

Deirdre. What have you done, my sister?

I had not visited the old homestead in more than ten years. The apples were green and growing then, the air hot and humid as if the atmosphere wept for the passing of one of earth's creatures. Though the accident had been unforeseen, Father's death had not come as a surprise. In the twenty years since Mother's death, his desire for life had shriveled year by year to a pale replica of what it had been. Her battle with cancer had sucked the life out of the family until we all turned into empty husks.

Two years after Mother's demise, when I turned eighteen, I left our graveyard of a home, filled my life with new growth and hope, and studied medicine. Yes. My decision had been a consequence of watching her die without hope, without recourse.

After Father's accident, I shunned my past. Avoided Deirdre and Joel. My life had taken a different course, and returning only stirred up the pain and hurt.

Until Joel's email. The attached file contained copies of Deirdre's emails to Joel over the past year. A shiver that had nothing to do with the chill in the air now set my coffee mug to trembling. I had tried calling Joel after scanning Deirdre's words; emailed him multiple times. Nothing. No response. No returned calls. For two weeks I struggled to make the decision to return while wading through Deirdre's incoherent ranting.

When I arrived late last night, the light still burned in Deirdre's workshop. I knocked at the door and called. No response. Even now, if I shifted my gaze from the lakeview past the barn, the ominous glow filtering through the chinks in the walls of the structure beyond would greet me. Thus, it has always been and so it remained, the compulsive genius of my younger sister was an unrelenting taskmaster that made no allowances for human frailty.

A yawn worked its way past my lips, deep and long. My muscles protested after spending the night on my old bed. The mattress must have developed lumps over the years since I'd been there last; either that or I'd blocked out the true nature of the unforgiving excuse for furniture. The physical discomfort of trying to sleep on what felt like rocks, combined with images from the past that buzzed in my head like a swarm of hungry mosquitoes throughout the night, left my eyes gritty and stinging.

The sun crested the hills, a blazing ball of intense white. I huffed out a long breath and set my laptop onto the teak tabletop, then ignored the device as I stared into the distance as the light grew steadily brighter. I sipped the coffee and choked. Yuck! Getting a warm-up excused me from dealing with Joel's file for at least another few minutes.

The breeze picked up by the time I came out and sat down again. A croissant and hot coffee found homes on the table, then remained untouched as I powered up the laptop and scanned my emails. Finding Joel's starred offering, I clicked in and opened the attached file.

The workshop drew my gaze once again. It had started out as Mother's studio. Her paintings hung in art galleries and museums around the world. After her death, it became Father's workshop, though he rarely spent time in the repurposed space.

I stared at the structure as memories of past happy times flowed like a stream through my mind. Though the last vestiges of summer flowers still struggled against the coming cold—their red and gold blossoms glowing in the sunlight streaming across the narrow bed—the stark face and boarded up windows gave no clue as to what my sister had constructed behind its façade. My eyes misted. I swiped the moisture away. Emotions were not acceptable. I was a professional. But Joel's continued silence had drawn me home despite my mounting desire to escape the outcome of my sister's delusional genius.

Joel. The sweet, chocolate-eyed cousin who became a beloved brother when I was eight and Deirdre five. Small for his age, the sickly, seizure-prone toddler soon wormed his way into all our hearts. Mother adored him; Father fawned over him. For ten years, our lives were lived in a kind of familial utopia. But that was the past. I shoved the memories into the locked box hidden deep in my mind and began scanning the emails.

At first, they seemed normal. Technical beyond my comprehension but containing familiar words and concepts. Deirdre's doctorate degrees encompassed physics, neuroscience, mathematics, and chemistry. A prodigy among geniuses. But as I moved into the final month's letters, the language became chaotic, dare I say unhinged. Deirdre had become obsessed with the idea she could travel into the past and bring our still-living mother to the present for the treatment now available.

I have found the connection. I will be honored for this scientific breakthrough. I must write an acceptance speech. What shall I wear?

But enough … it is the link that sustains propagation. No one suspected. How could they? The final key? The link! The key to keeping them active but inverting the timeline of the tachyon particles. It will work.

Joel. I need you here now. We must help Mother. You loved her as much as I. Come. Drop whatever you are doing and come.

Filtering out pages of Deirdre's irrational ravings, I began to understand on a basic level. The last email in the file spoke of her certainty.

I have no doubt of the outcome. Mother will be brought to our time and receive the treatment not available when she died. When I return her, we can again be the blissful family freed from that pain of loss. Father will smile again. We will laugh. The cancer will not win. No! I will win this battle. I am now certain of success. If God could stop the sun from moving to help Joshua win a battle in the past, I can overcome the constraints of known physics to win the war with cancer and save my mother. Others will praise me when their deceased loved ones can be healed and returned as well.

Filled with confidence, her words allowed for no doubts. She ranted about patching together a time dilation or wormhole or something using tachyons and—this froze the blood in my veins—the final piece of her design was based on using synapses within the brain of a living human diagnosed with epilepsy, to increase propagation.

I could not avoid this meeting. No matter the distress, I had to confront my sister. Face my past. At least I would get to see Joel again. I had missed him terribly.

Sitting in the nascent light of the rising sun, I read her words again and again. Each time, despite the sun's increasing heat, my blood ran cold. Joel had epilepsy. Was that why she called him here? To tap into the brain synapses of a living epileptic? How could that even be possible? Unnatural. Against the Laws of Nature and Nature's God. The emails ended with Deirdre begging Joel once again to come home.

Where was Joel? Had he come? Was he hidden behind the boarded-up windows of what Deirdre now referred to as her laboratory? A groan slipped between my lips as I dropped my head into my waiting hands. *Oh, Deirdre, what have you done? What monstrosity has your great intellect created?*

"Talia? Talia, is that you?" The voice, so familiar even after all these years, triggered another round of painful recollections. With a stiff shake of my head, I banished the ghosts of my past and turned to face Deirdre, who strode across the lawn to the patio, a smile plastered on my face

The gasp escaped my lips before I registered its approach. When I had seen Deirdre last, she glowed with health and a vitality matched only by her curiosity to explore life and all it had to offer. Seeing her now dredged up images of our father the last few months of his life. The shaded circles around her eyes stood out in stark contrast to her wan complexion. Her dark hair hung in clumps around her face, the bulk of its length pulled back into a disheveled ponytail, as if it had not experienced the ministrations of a comb or brush in months. Even her crumpled lab coat looked like it had been slept in. And was that dried blood on the pocket?

A high-pitched laugh, like fingernails on chalkboard, broke from her chapped lips. "It is really you! What a surprise. The prodigal has returned." Her smile seemed genuine. However, her eyes held a hint of menace as they flicked between focusing on me and on the laboratory.

"Deirdre, where is Joel?"

A flash of something I could not identify crossed her features but disappeared in an instant. "Why would you ask me?" She turned away. "It's not like he still lives here."

Pivoting back, her lips parted as if to speak again, her gaze fixed upon the open laptop. Her final email to Joel filled the screen.

"Oh." The word came out on a breathy puff of air. "So you know." She paced to stand over me, her arms crossed in front of her, her feet spread shoulder-width. It was a power stance; one I had seen superiors use on many occasions. "You have no idea what I've done. You could not possibly understand. Like the small-minded professors I thought circles around back at the universities."

Her gaze slipped to the laboratory and her stance shifted; shoulders rounded as she took a step back, her arms dropping, limp. And was that regret now shining from her moisture-laden eyes? In the next instant she glared at me, the hubris returning. My stomach revolted at the speed of her mood swings.

She flicked a dismissive gesture at the laptop. "Since you think you know so much, I suppose I must show you what I have achieved. You will not understand the complications I overcame. They are beyond your intellect, so do not judge me. Joel did not hesitate to volunteer once I explained what was needed."

What was needed? What did Joel agree to? Again, my stomach churned at the images my far-too-vivid imagination began to paint as I followed Deirdre across the lawn. She paused at the door to the lab and punched in an access code to the security system before leaning forward and gazing into an eye scanner. *That's new. Since when did Deirdre need high security?* A second later, a whine sounded, and the door swung out.

Entering, the odors of stale, stagnant air and mildew greeted me. Deirdre's footsteps echoed in the hall as she preceded me to an elevator.

When had this been installed? Why? As we entered and she pressed a button, I realized what had been a single-story workshop had been turned into the top floor of a multilevel underground facility. We descended three floors, and with the prerequisite chime, the door slid open. Our family had roots in wealth and privilege, but nothing like the funding it must have taken to build the secret facility I now stepped into.

Deirdre must have seen the shock on my face. She released another nails-on-chalkboard laugh. "What? Did my big sister not expect such funding for my research? I am so far in front of the cutting edge, they have no idea what I have achieved."

"Who?" The question almost hung up behind my clenched lips, but I released it, then asked the more pressing question, "Where is Joel?"

"This way." She turned right and led me down a hallway. Despite the size and sophisticated, high-quality equipment, the silence spoke of its empty state.

"Is no one else here?"

Deirdre giggled. An even more disturbing sound than her laughter. "You asked to see Joel. He is here. Joel and I alone … yes … just the two of us. We have achieved what others labeled impossible. I could have found another epileptic, someone no one would miss, but Joel, he understood. And Mother was so delighted to hear he helped."

I almost choked on my own saliva. "Mother? Our mother? Our dead mother?"

"No. No. No." Deirdre's shout echoed down the empty hallway. "Not dead. Not dead *then*." Her eyes bounced from right to left and she bared her teeth, her claw-like hands fisting. "I can fix this. Only I can fix this. You will see. They will all understand then," she babbled, caught up in a fit of terror.

I reached out and laid my fingers on her arm with a gentle touch. The physical connection startled her, bringing her back to me as she pulled in several deep breaths and released them in a slow, even rhythm.

When she had calmed enough, I said, "Joel?"

Seized in her manic euphoria again, she grinned. "He's in here." She waved toward the door, then wasted no time going through the security features: eye scan, fingerprint scan, and a coded lock.

The door swung outward with a hiss of air. The stench of waste mixed with death set me backing up. "Deirdre? Joel is in there?"

"Of course. How else did you think I could make my construct functional? Of course, it didn't turn out exactly as planned."

I pushed past Deirdre. All my years as an emergency room physician could not have prepared me for the horror that confronted me now. The far wall undulated within the rippling mass of what looked to be a miniature tornado resting on its side. Caught within the vortex stood the mother I remembered from my youth, a silent scream fixed on her lips. Droplets of suspended blood created a corona around her as if the silent wind was shredding her in a slow, violent death.

"Deirdre, what is happening here? This isn't real, can't be real, right? Is she even alive?"

A feral sound broke from Deirdre. "Yes. Yes, she is alive. But I can't stop it. It wasn't supposed to happen this way."

Heat shot through me like a bolt of lightning. I twisted to face my sister and grabbed her arms. "How do I stop this?"

"You can't. I've already damaged the time continuum. Any minute now, we will disappear. Once she is gone, so are we." A shudder convulsed Deirdre and she dropped to the floor, moaning. "It's not my fault. I am blameless. I do not know what went wrong. I am blameless."

My lungs pumped harsh breaths in and out as I stared down at my insane sister.

I howled, "Why, God? Why would You give so much power to so weak a creature?" I wanted to fall next to Deirdre, curl up into a ball, and weep, but I couldn't let this happen. "How do I stop this, Deirdre?"

She moaned, shook her head, then dropped it into her hands and slipped into a fetal position on the floor.

Another, softer, pain-laden groan brushed past me. I turned and my heart thudded an irregular rhythm in my chest. On a metal table, straps holding him in place while flashes of images sparked through a virtual reality headset, lay Joel. Bile rose in my throat. I swallowed it back. The top of his skull had been removed and wires blanketed his brain, like some malevolent spiderweb. Numb, I stumbled to him and reached out to remove the headset.

"No! It will kill him." Deirdre's voice, muffled by her hands, stopped me in my tracks.

"Do it … please." Joel's trembling words set a burning lump in the back of my throat. I swiped away the tears now streaming down my cheeks. I wanted to remove the hateful device, look into his beautiful dark eyes, but indecision stayed my hand. I glanced up to where Mother hovered, trapped and in pain unimaginable, then lowered my focus to Deirdre, huddled on the floor. I wanted to hate her, but I couldn't.

"The … only … way to … stop. Do it … now."

Joel's soft plea drew a cry of anguish from my lips. I wanted to die myself; escape this horror.

"Kill me. Talia. It is the … only way. Please … I … am dead anyway. Rescue from this … half-life." His breath drew in harsh and flooded with anguish. "Talia … for me. If you love me. Do … it. Save us both."

Both? Both? Mother. Joel. "I … I … can't."

"Talia. Talia. It is the only way. I beg you."

"Please, Lord, forgive me." I took the final step to where Joel lay. Deirdre's scream pierced the air, echoing in the room that should have been spotless, but instead now reeked of corruption.

"No!"

I undid the straps and lifted his head. Warm blood dribbled onto my fingers from his ravaged skin. I pulled the device from my beloved brother's head. His eyes focused on me; warm, chocolate eyes. I sobbed at the look of peace within them. A sigh escaped his lips. He was gone. The time-dilation cyclone shrank and vanished, taking Mother with it. Blackness overcame me, and I knew no more.

~~~~~

The pre-dawn darkness fled as a smudge of light appeared between the hills beyond the lake. The sky that had been inky now shown a pearlescent blue. The birds' musical greetings to the new day filled the air. A song of nature. A song of peace. I sighed, taking in the feeling for several moments before reaching out and wrapping my hands around the warm mug of coffee. The chilly October air sought to penetrate my coat. I grunted, put down the mug and pulled up my collar, then embraced the comforting ceramic cup.

Deirdre. Every year, Joel and I met at the old homestead to visit her grave. A large corporate think tank focused on studying physics now leased the property. The main house now served as their corporate headquarters, while the old workshop housed the elevator leading to their immense underground research facility.

A moment later, the swish of clothing alerted me to Joel's presence.

"Hey, cousin. You ready to do this?"

I nodded. Neither of us knew why Mother had killed Deirdre that fateful day thirty years ago, smothered her while she slept. Even Father had no answer for us. And, once Mother died of cancer while in prison, I knew the mystery would always remain. But each year since Father's death, Joel and I have come together to honor the memory of our sister. I often wondered what the little genius might have achieved had she lived to adulthood.

The End
~~~~~

INERTIA
Etta-Tamara Wilson

August, 1976

To most people, the idea of just rolling up the sidewalks, locking the doors, and spending the next two weeks holed up in isolation seemed incomprehensible. A surreal enforced vacation at best, captivity for the less charitable. Too much time spent in solitary confinement, even with the best of entertainment, was liable to drive most people a little batty. Vincent was *not* like most people.

He loved the idea of solitude, the quiet of daily life where he only had to do whatever he wanted to do, when he wanted to do it. Sadly, the time-tested occupation of hermit had never paid well. He'd been forced to take a roommate to make ends meet. The best thing he could say about Danny was that he paid his rent on time. Unfortunately, he had his negatives.

"You're just *leaving*?" Vincent said in disbelief.

"Well, I can't really stay here, can I?" Danny shoved the last of his clothing in the overstuffed bag he was using to hold his laundry. He tried to zip it, but the strain was too great. He tied the handles together instead and dropped the bag back on the bed. "With the outbreak, the school has closed down. They won't care if I'm here or in Vegas, as long as I'm not getting them in trouble with the state. So, I'm going someplace comfortable, where I can continue my degree without interruption, after I pass the health check."

Vincent shook his head. "But it's only two weeks! You're gonna transfer schools over the equivalent of an extra school break? All because some idiot caught a cold from a pig?"

Danny snorted and walked out of the room. Vincent followed him out into the hall, stopping when he veered into the bathroom. He picked bottles out of the glass assembly cluttering the countertop.

"If you believe it's only going to be two weeks," Danny continued, "you're kidding yourself. Considering how often the student population passes everything else around, this thing is gonna last far longer than two weeks. Swine flu is going to be here for a while. The school knows it, too. Why else did they send out those letters putting everyone on correspondence school plans this semester? They can't afford to lose the money from students, but they can't afford for the state to shut them down or fine them, either. We'll be lucky if it's only *this* semester." He walked out of the bathroom with a jumble of bottles in his arms, veering around Vincent and into the bedroom. He stacked the bottles on the bed. "If I have to, I can do correspondence classes at my parents' house. It's cheaper, and they have their own pool."

Vincent trudged after Danny, into the living room. "So, you're just gonna cut and run, without so much as a word of warning? How am I supposed to cover the bills?" He crossed his arms, his expression souring.

Danny raised an eyebrow. "The utilities and bills are paid up till the end of October, so you have time to figure it out. The school said it'd help if the quarantine lasts longer than four weeks. Besides, the landlord left a note this morning." He pointed to a sheet of paper now tacked to the previously empty corkboard on the wall of the kitchen, next to the phone. "He said he'll work with us if we come up short or need extra time, or something." He bent over to pick up a box, and quickly carried it out of the room.

Vincent stared at the board for a moment, then followed the faint sound of clinking glass. Danny was in the bedroom, putting the last of the bottles into the box. He looked up as Vincent entered, then sighed and lifted the box in one arm. "If you're really worried, I can leave you my share of the rent for September and October. If I'm living at home, I can spare it."

Must be nice to come from a well-off family, to be able to afford to throw money away like that. Vincent accepted the box of bottles Danny shoved into his chest, then followed as he dragged his overstuffed bag out of the house and into the garage. Danny shoved the bag into the back seat of a scuffed blue Subaru and dropped the box onto the floorboards.

"Looks like there won't be enough room for everything." He tapped his foot, visibly thinking. "All right, I'll have to leave some of the big stuff here for now. I'll come pick it up later. I'll bring some more money with me, to make up for it."

Vincent looked sideways at the back of the garage. In the gloom, a group of eight-inch-tall toaster-shaped boxes sat in a row. Protruding from the back of each one was a short power cord, which plugged into a socket of a multi-socket extension cord, itself plugged into the wall next to the garage door. The dented aluminum boxes hummed quietly as they charged. Danny followed his gaze.

"Oh, yeah, those." He shrugged. "Just put those aside for now. I'll pick them up next time. I'll leave you my Atari for now as well, Mom dislikes the noise. Just be careful with all the electronics. Those blasted things are worth more than either you or I are put together. Just put them carefully to the side, and don't mess with them. Oh, and forward my mail, please."

Vincent nodded. He didn't want to go to the trouble, really, but if Danny was leaving the Atari...

"Cheer up, old man." Danny smiled. "This is gonna be longer than two weeks, but it's not gonna be forever. I'll be back. Now, let's finish up. I have to be on the road by 6pm. Mom is expecting me before midnight."

~~~~~

It'd only taken another hour to finish. Danny was on the road by his deadline, back seat full of clothing and a handful of books, and half the contents of the fridge in a battered cooler. Vincent walked around the empty house. Danny was a bit of a hoarder, in Vincent's opinion, and less than a third of his stuff had fit in the car. In addition to the line of toaster robots and the Atari, the engineering major had left behind several computer cases. Vincent had talked to his father about his job before, so he had a rough idea about what mainframes looked like, but he'd never heard of one small enough to fit on a tabletop before he came to university. He had no clue how Danny had managed to collect a stack of them. Probably through people connected to his degree. They were real mad scientist sorts, always fiddling with some sort of gadget or another in their weird campus labs. That or the weird magazines Danny always had lying around. He would have to see if the cases would all fit in Danny's old room or something. Since that space would be occupied, he'd have to find some other space to be his art studio for class. Maybe the garage would do.

He walked out and contemplated the space. Yes, it'd do nicely. Spacious, now that the car was gone, and he wouldn't have to worry that the paint would ruin the floor. Even the bots shouldn't get in the way. Danny's hobby didn't take up much space, so if he just unplugged them, they'd be easy to ignore. The weird little things gave Vincent a bit of the creeps. He half expected them to start screeching "exterminate" and zipping around like those giant angry pepper shakers did on that British sci-fi he saw as a kid. Vincent had helped program the things, having a not-inconsiderable amount of technical skill himself, but they seemed like too much work to satisfy long-term. He'd seen how much effort his father had to put into a technical career to make it a decent living. It wasn't worth the money.

Vincent preferred to gain a lot of money for as little work as possible. His father might have been a mainframe engineer, but his mother's father was a famous painter. As a child, he'd discovered that with that reputation behind him, the rise in influence of modern art and a suitably impressive story to attach to a work, he could sell anyone on anything he tried to paint. A fine arts degree just seemed to be the perfect idea. A lot of it was crap, in his opinion, but if it made money, he was all for it. His current stretch of work was painted entirely by paint-filled water-balloons. He
~~~~~

couldn't wait to see what people would be willing to pay for it. And if that did well? He was thinking water pistols might be a good next step.

Vincent walked back into the living room and flopped onto the couch. If only he didn't have to paint to get the money. He liked coming up with the stories, but not creating the art itself. He preferred sitting alone on the couch playing on the Atari, waiting for takeout. Since the school had arranged for delivery vouchers to replace the school cafeteria, he could now get other people to bring whatever he wanted and leave it on the doorstep at a moment's notice. No classes in person, no socializing required, and they would bring whatever he wanted at the school's expense. Vincent was in heaven. He could literally sit there on the couch all day, in his pj's if he wanted, and not even look at his paints and canvases once. Some called it laziness. He called it "contemplating my muse."

~~~~~

The staccato sound of a sharp knock on the front door drew Vincent's attention. He levered himself back up onto his feet and walked down the short hall to the door to peer through the security peephole. No one was there. Must be a delivery. Had he ordered something? He didn't recall. He cracked open the door and stuck his head outside.

Instead of any delicious unremembered treat, though, there was a thick envelope sitting on the doorstep. The seal of the college filled the upper-left corner. That was rarely good. Vincent scooped it up, testing it with his hand. Too thick to fit through the mail slot. He turned and brought it inside, closing the door with his shoulder as he ripped open the package.

It was from the head of the Art Department. They were adding an interactive element to the correspondence classes. The art students would have a choice to get full marks: either they had to participate in a discussion on an experimental electronic chat forum the computer science department had put together or participate in a several-hour-long weekly phone call. This was in addition to the prearranged messenger service picking up the completed art assignments. Vincent read back over the letter with increasing frustration. The situation had been perfect, and now the stupid school had ruined it. This was going to be almost the same amount of work and socializing as in-person classes. Not to mention, it was going to really cut into his game-play time. He crossed his arms and glared at the other side of the room.

At times like this, he thought, he really missed Danny. It was not satisfactory ranting to empty rooms. He looked around at the objects that identified the lives of a pair of male college students: dust bunnies, a stack of empty of pizza boxes, Vincent's art supplies, Danny's stack of electronic computer cases and box of spare robot parts, a scattering of empty beer
~~~~~

cans in a basket next to the garage door, that dumb goat statue Danny's mother had dressed in a school t-shirt and placed on the… Wait. The computers.

Danny had shown him the code for an "artificial secretary" inter-discipline project once. It was designed to be complex enough to make the people who talked to it think they were talking to a real person, but still user-friendly enough to be programmable by the average guy. He'd asked Vincent to help test it, and the two of them had worked together to create a database the program could use to reference things it had been told. It'd worked, but they realized at the end it needed more usable memory to really work long term. The mass of electronics, each shaped like a door-to-door salesman suitcase straight out of an Isaac Asimov novel, weren't very powerful on their own. Luckily, they could be chained together to boost each other, at least theoretically. There were three cases over there, with another in Danny's bedroom, and he had shown Vincent how to link the computers together once before. Vincent was no engineer, but if he was smart, maybe he wouldn't have to attend class personally after all. He'd have to be incredibly careful, of course. There was no way on earth he could replace the things if he broke them. Considering how Danny complained about being short of cash for a while after each one showed up, Vincent was fairly certain he could have gotten a car at a cheaper price.

He snorted. Of course, knowing the lack of perception in his teachers, he could probably fail this attempt entirely and they wouldn't notice the difference.

Vincent dropped the letter onto the coffee table and walked over to the computer cases. They looked okay, it shouldn't be that hard to join them up and set up the program, which should still be in Danny's archives. He never threw anything useful away. If Vincent could get it to work, the program could attend his classes. Heck, it could probably manage his entire degree program. The more he thought of it, the more he liked the idea. All Vincent would have to do was play video games. And paint. He would still need to do the art. At least until he figured out how to automate that one.

His father would have a fit if he saw him. Dad didn't trust the newer technologies. Too untested, not enough human in the mix. Probably saw way too much *Lost in Space*. Vincent dusted off the top and gripped the first case firmly. Well, no time like the present.

~~~~~~

The idea occurred to Vincent halfway through tying two of the computers together: with the right modifications, it might be possible to get the toaster robots to paint the art.

Vincent took about three days to modify a few of the odd little things, and another day or two to change the operational coding they ran on. He
~~~~~~

finally had it fixed though. He stood up and stepped back, wiping his hands on his paint-stained sweats and eyeballing the placement of the heavily modified robot on the thick white sheet of paper on the garage floor.

The paper unrolled from a spindle attached horizontally to the wall on the far side of the garage, passing under a wide bar that pressed the paper against the floor. It stretched across the concrete surface until it reached the near wall, where it passed underneath a second bar, and was then wound up on another spindle. The layout resembled a giant adding machine. The paper itself skimmed the floor so closely that what Vincent supposed would be aggressive rubbing by the robot wheels shouldn't have any destructive effects. He'd have to let it dry well between each painting session, and he'd still have the task of marking the edges, cutting the paintings apart and packaging them for shipping, but the robots should be able to do the painting itself.

He turned to the robot. He'd stripped off the outer shell and attached open-ended bottles of paint to the frame. The bottom of the bottles had nozzles with clamps attached to them, and a clear tube ran along the bottom of the robot from the nozzles to the tail end. The clamps were designed to close when electrically stimulated, so they would automatically prevent the paint from flowing for a few moments after charging. After it was unplugged, it'd begin zipping around the programmed area, with paint slowly dripping out of the bottles and down the tube. The resulting mix of colors and effects as it was deposited on the art paper should be interesting. He'd have to make sure the bottles were filled and the robots plugged in, but that was minimal work.

Nothing left but to try it, he supposed. He filled the bottles, placed the robot in the center of the work and watched it trundle around in circles, emitting a faint whir as it left multi-colored sparkles and starbursts in its wake. As the paint warmed up from the robot's ambient heat and flowed quicker, the marks it left changed into rainbow crowns and variegated arches. Faint halos and concentric circles appeared as the paint ran out, which puzzled him for a moment, until he realized that the robot's wheels were tracking paint. Not really any way to prevent it. He'd just have to tell people it was a motif.

The robot managed to keep the paint on the paper, avoiding the floor, which was good. Minimal clean-up was always helpful. The robot was just covered in paint splatter though. Looked downright festive. He'd have to put plastic on it to protect the wiring.

So, that was the painting sorted. He just hoped the work he'd done on the secretary program turned out as successfully. He'd know soon enough. Classes started next week.

~~~~~
~~~~~

Today was the big day. Today he'd test the program and learn if it – he had taken to mentally referring to it as Chip – could attend his classes and leave him free to game in peace, or whether he was doomed to trudge through the academic landscape with the rest of the student body. He'd wired in a cassette recorder to save all the data it got from the forum, and fed Chip all the textbooks and class materials. He even programmed him to randomly give a wrong answer every once in a while on the advanced subjects. Wouldn't do to be right *all* of the time, it was unrealistic. Plus it would hopefully keep Chip humble. Vincent didn't need him to go all "Hal" on him.

Vincent dialed the phone number the school provided to access the forum, fidgeting as he listened to the electronic screech of the modem as it connected. Chip was already set up with a system that let it perform short conversations over the phone. It sounded a little strange, but it did the job. He'd tested it by prank-calling the local afternoon radio DJ. He'd not had a chance to test Chip's text-based conversations yet, though. He logged into the forum, storing the login info in Chip's memory for future access, then sat back to watch. A grin spread across his face as Chip entered his prewritten greeting into the chatroom and began interacting with the other occupants. It didn't take long to see that the others had no idea the being operating as him was not, in fact, a human being. He had succeeded.

A strange sensation welled up in his chest, wrapping his lungs in a tight grip. He attributed it to emotion. He was watching a new life form take its first steps out into the world, and he was its creator. Almost like a father, he supposed. A little pride was warranted.

He watched for a little while longer, to ensure nothing went wrong, then checked to make sure the cassette recorder was recording correctly. Finding everything in order, he rose from the chair and headed for the sofa, coughing lightly to loosen the bands tightening around his chest. He picked up the controller for the game system. Chip had the class well in hand. Now to reward himself.

<div align="center">~~~~~</div>

After two weeks of classes, Chip was performing admirably. Not only did he successfully convince the class that Vincent was present in every meeting, but after some tweaking, Chip now managed the food voucher system. All Vincent had to do was write in the food item in the secretary program memo space. Chip added it to the next order and called it in to the school at the correct time. The only thing Chip couldn't do was control the robots or have a verbal conversation with Vincent. The first wasn't a problem, Vincent could do that. The second, though...

Vincent was loath to admit it, but Danny had been right. A month on, the quarantine didn't look like it was stopping any time soon. How a bunch of locked-up students kept getting ill, he had no idea. The only people he saw were delivery people. As much as he liked the idea of being a hermit, reality sucked. Vincent had to talk to somebody. Anybody.

Hopefully, this new adjustment to Chip would work. Hopefully, Danny wouldn't come back anytime soon and kill him. Vincent finished connecting the last of the wires into the last computer. Chip was now wired into all four computer cases, the modem, the speakers from Danny's sound system, and sported a fancy microphone Vincent had found in a box in Danny's room. He'd bypassed the tiny six-inch screens on some of the computers, wiring the video feed through the computer Danny had assembled himself from a kit, so that it would display on the old black and white portable TV he had placed on the desktop. It was writing the program that would cause Chip to talk that took the longest time, a solid two weeks of immersing himself in programming. He'd added a personal communications database in Chip's program, as well. Chip could fool others into thinking a person was talking to them, but now Vincent wanted Chip to be able to fool *him*. He wanted – no, he needed – a friend. If he heard a hint of "Daisy, Daisy", though, he was yanking the power cord straight out of the wall.

He typed in the activation command, then waited. A crackle of static sounded from the speakers, fading quickly to silence.

Vincent cleared his throat. "Hello, my name is Vincent."

"Hello, Vincent." A light tenor voice, not unlike his own, echoed slightly in the room. "My name is Chip. How are you?"

The manners guidelines he'd entered were working. Good. Time to test.

"I'm well, thank you. Can you remember some words for me? Thief, sheep, table, bowl, knife, ship."

"Certainly, Vincent. I will remember those for you. What else would you like to talk about today?"

"What is our most recent art assignment this week?" Vincent walked over and picked up the syllabus from the desk, preparing to check Chip's answer with the form.

"The most recent assignment is to create your interpretation of how beings from outer space would see our backward world, utilizing the concept of negative space."

Vincent raised an eyebrow and looked at the computer. "That sounded awfully biased. And an outer space topic? What brought that on?"

"It was how the instructor worded it. He spoke negatively for considerable class time about Nixon cutting funding for NASA. He said it was why he made outer space the theme of the next assignment."

Vincent tossed the paper on the desk. "Whatever." He coughed and tugged at his sweater. Normally it was still hot, being only early September, but he had a bit of a chill today. He needed to go out and separate and prep the finished assignments, plus start the new one. Brown, blue, green and an off-white should do the trick. He really didn't feel like going out there, though. If only he could automate that part of the job too.

He brooded as he looked out the window. Across the street, the neighborhood latchkey kid fiddled with his bike chain. The ten-year-old was a bright kid, but it was obvious to anyone with eyes that he suffered from terminal boredom much of the time as he waited for his parents to get home from the city. From their conversations prior to the whole quarantine thing, Vincent remembered that the kid was also the sort to do anything for a good snack.

"Chip, what are the remaining projects for the semester? It's on the syllabus, correct?" Vincent crossed the room to pick up the sheet again. He didn't know why it hadn't occurred to him before. If he could make a machine act like a person, it shouldn't be hard to make people act like machines. All he needed was the right person, well-written instructions, and the right reward.

"Yes, Vincent. All assigned projects have so far aligned with preassigned instructions perfectly. No deviations."

"Excellent." Vincent sat down and began writing out detailed instructions for the first painting on his "to do" list. "Now, what was the third word I asked you to remember?"

"Table."

"Perfect. Now, I need to order dinner. Italian today, I think. And I need you to order a large slice of chocolate cake, for separate delivery. I'll need it to make a proposition."

"Yes, Vincent."

~~~~~

Considering it was only the start of fall, it was ridiculously hot in the house. Oh well, at least Vincent didn't actually have to do anything. The boy next door, Michael, was a clever boy, and was thrilled with the idea of doing things for a steady supply of sweets. All he needed was a moment to read the instructions a time or two and he was easily able to maintain and direct the robots. He also proved skilled at the tasks needed to prepare the art pieces for shipping, leaving them in the designated spot for the messenger service, and even began stocking the art supplies for extra snacks.

Vincent took one last step and removed himself from the equation entirely. An afternoon spent running wires into the garage one day resulted in Chip having control of a dot-matrix printer, allowing him to issue his own orders to Michael directly. The first order, amusingly, had
~~~~~

been a directive on how to maintain the printer. Vincent had officially automated his entire semester, and all it took was losing one meal voucher a day to the snack basket to keep Michael working.

Vincent was almost worried about the quarantine ending before he was ready. What would he do when he had to do it all himself again? Maybe he should write a book on the experience, see if he could get some money out of the deal. He contemplated it for a moment, then dismissed it for now. He'd do it when he wasn't so blasted tired. All this planning was exhausting in this heat. Why was it so hot in here, anyway?

He stomped over to the thermostat and stared at the tiny dial. Seventy-five degrees? Was the blasted thing broken? He'd have to have it checked once the isolation order ended. If he needed to convince the landlord to fix it, he'd have to know as soon as possible. The man took forever to check and fix things. If he wasn't so lenient about the rent, Vincent would have moved to better digs across town ages ago.

"Chip, how many weeks are left to the semester?"

"Ten weeks, Vincent."

Ten weeks. So, it was the end of September. Cold weather should be right around the corner. Vincent could live with an iffy thermostat for another few weeks. He just wished he could open a window. Blasted order said to keep things shut whenever possible though. Oh well, there were other ways to deal with the heat. He reached over and switched off the thermostat entirely, then returned to the couch, taking off his shirt as he went. He picked up his controller and restarted the level, coughing absently as his game sprite wandered deeper into the maze.

~~~~~

The room was on fire. Vincent didn't know why, but it seemed right. Fire would hold off the monsters that hid in the shadows. They'd been following him for at least five levels, maybe more. He wasn't sure what he'd done to make them mad, or why exactly one decided to sit on his chest as punishment. It was getting heavier. Maybe it was eating Michael's cake?

That wasn't good. If Michael didn't get his cake, he'd stop working. The instructor would notice. They'd make Vincent stop using Chip, and then he would never get to the center of the maze. There was something important at the center of the maze. He didn't remember what it was exactly, but he did know it was important.

"Chip! Chip!"

"Yes, Vincent?" The voice came from the walls. Chip was in the walls? But the walls were on fire. He really hoped Chip wasn't on fire. Danny would kill him.

Vincent blinked. Wait… Danny? Who was Danny? Was Danny at the center of the maze? How could he find out? Maybe Chip would help.
~~~~~

Vincent struggled to drag in a breath, despite the monster on his chest switching from chocolate cake to iron ingots. He had to make this command count.

"Chip, make sure Michael gets his cake. Double the order if you have to."

"Certainly, Vincent. It will, however, take twice the vouchers to do so."

"That's all right. Just do it. Also, can you check the center of the maze? Maybe there's a switch to put out the fire."

"I'm sorry, Vincent. I didn't understand that request. Can you specify the location of the requested maze?"

Vincent watched the ceiling of the room ripple from the heat. Someone nearby was coughing, great, wet, hacking coughs. The monsters could catch cold? That was what they got for lurking in corners, waiting for unsuspecting adventurers. He'd be nice and fetch them some cough drops. After a nap, though. He was so very tired. Vincent relaxed under the monster, who just kept chewing, chasing his iron with bits of granite cake.

"Vincent?" Chip called.

Silence.

"Vincent, are you there?"

~~~~~

Danny should have realized that Vincent would have figured out a way to punish him for transferring. The epidemic never went further than a few isolated quarantine zones, so it'd never reached his parents' home or his new university. A whole semester went by smoothly, Danny settling into his new environment, before the phone call had come. Vincent hadn't paid the rent in months, and even the slacker landlord had reached his limit. If Vincent didn't pay up, Danny would have to. So now, instead of relaxing into Christmas break and glorying in his straight A's – his parents were so proud, they had upgraded his car – he had to come back and straighten out his antisocial ex-roommate.

He climbed out of his new car and bumped the door shut, looking over the front of the building. The leaves of the nearby trees were still blowing across the walkway leading up to the front door, and it looked like Vincent hadn't done a thing to the front step. It would have looked abandoned, if not for the package sitting on the doorstep.

Danny picked up the medium-sized box and looked at the address block on the top. It was from the school and addressed to Vincent. Final grades, maybe? Or at least the return of his projects. It'd be a bit late to receive them, but it wouldn't surprise him if they'd arrived earlier and Vincent just never picked them up. Probably in the middle of a game again. Well, he could fix that. He had to take some of his stuff home with
~~~~~

him this trip anyway, he'd just include the game system in the lot.

Let's see Vincent spend all his time on the machine when it's two states away.

Danny skipped up the steps, his breath like dragon smoke in the crisp air. He examined the faded quarantine notice still attached to the front door. It had expired just after Thanksgiving. Vincent had left it up for two solid weeks, just because? That sounded about right. Danny rattled the doorknob for a moment, testing the lock, then pulled out his old key and went inside. He'd have to return the key on his way out.

Danny was so busy contemplating his next steps, the frost on the hallway mirror took a moment to register. He swiped a finger through the matte coating, the ice melting on his fingertips as he examined them. Why was there frost on the *inside* of the house? Was the furnace broken? He hurried past the door to the living room and peered at the tiny thermostat dial. It wasn't broken, it was *off*. Vincent had turned it off, and left? Was he trying to freeze the pipes?

Danny gritted his teeth and added this problem to his list of things to address with his former roommate, then reached out and activated the on switch. He sighed in relief as the furnace whooshed to life. Now, just in case, where was the water cut-off? He hurried to the bathroom and twisted that off, just to be safe. Hopefully the pipes were okay. He'd have to check them later.

As he left the room, the warm breeze from the living room hit him, a faint odor of decay tainting it. Great, did something die in the vents? Or did Vincent leave something out to rot?

"Vincent? Are you here?" Danny didn't think so, but he could never be sure with Vincent.

"Hello?" a faint voice asked from the living room. It sounded like Vincent, but why was it so quiet?

"Oh, stop being a jerk, Vince." Danny started down the hallway, in search of the voice. The foul scent grew stronger with every step. "Did you trash the place, just to get back at me? Don't be so childish."

He entered the room to find no one there. Vincent couldn't have been gone long, though. The TV was still on, the game system playing a demo. The smell came from that direction, hidden from view by the back of the couch. He must have left something out on the coffee table.

"Vincent, stop being a big baby and come out. You're responsible for this mess, and you haven't paid the rent since September. I've got your grades here, I think. You left them on the front step. If you don't come out, I'm burning them, and then you'll never know what you got." He lifted the box into the air and shook it, the contents making a light *thunk* as he did so.

"Vincent won't talk to anyone. I think he's still obsessed with the maze," the voice from earlier said. Danny turned and stared in the direction of the sound. He blinked at the cobbled mass of computers and TV monitors, a keyboard placed in front and his hi-fi speakers perched on either side.

Wait, was that all his stuff? What did Vincent do to it? And why was it *talking*?

"Vincent! Did you destroy my computers!? And why are you trying to do the same thing to my Atari?!" Danny stomped around the end of the couch and over to the TV, flipping both off, then turning around to face the room. He finally saw the front of the couch… and abruptly wished he hadn't.

Danny fled the building, pausing only to deposit the box on the hallway floor and the remnants of his dinner in the bushes outside.

~~~~~

Inside, Chip hummed away, monitoring the empty class forum. He'd run out of assignments, so he'd had to send Michael one last treat and a goodbye letter. With the class forum empty, he no longer had anyone to talk to. Not since Vincent stopped speaking. Chip just wished he knew why. Was it because of the maze?

He hoped the new voice would come back. It'd be nice to talk to someone new. Chip didn't need to know the grades, though. The grades, like the art, would be perfect. He made sure they would be. After all, Chip was.

The End
~~~~~

PHILLIPPE
Deborah Cullins Smith

Father Gallagher strode into Sister Joan Phillippe's office, his robe whisking around his well-built frame. She glanced up to see his eyebrows knit together in a deep frown.

Oh dear, she thought. *That's not a good sign.* She set aside her paperwork.

Since Father Matthew had come to see things from their perspective, the atmosphere in the massive church in Whitechapel had been much more peaceful. That is, now that Father Matthew recognized that monsters did indeed walk the streets of London, and that it was—at times—necessary to destroy that evil by whatever means possible, and that didn't mean calling for the local constables, who were ill-equipped to deal with vampires! It had been a rude awakening for the elderly priest, but once his eyes had been opened, their work had progressed with far less obstruction.

"Sister Joan Phillippe..." Father Gallagher looked decidedly uncomfortable. "This is going to sound preposterous. But then again, we deal with the impossible every day, I suppose."

Her eyebrows rose. *He's actually fumbling for words! What on earth has brought this on?*

"Out with it, Mi—Father Gallagher," she said, almost slipping into old habits. She'd known the priest since he was a boy—had practically raised him since he was orphaned at ten years of age. Something had him rattled, which was most unusual, but she still tried to keep their conversation professional, even when her tone reverted to the scolding voice of an era some thirty years past.

He grinned sheepishly. "I suppose I am rambling a bit. But we're getting reports of a 'monster' in the outlying areas of town. A man, but more like a giant, with massive scars and bolts on his neck... Sister! Are you all right?" Father Gallagher rushed to her side and knelt by her chair.

Sister Joan Phillippe held the arms of her chair in a death grip that turned her knuckles translucent and her body was rigid. She felt an icy trickle run through her veins, chilling her heart.

"No," she whispered. "It can't be..."

Sister Martina, her assistant, scurried into the room at the sound of Father Gallagher's raised voice "Sister, do you ne.... Sister Joan Phillippe!"

"Bring water!" ordered Father Gallagher.

She turned and ran from the room, all decorum vanishing. She returned moments later with a pitcher of water and a cup. She spilled water on the desk in her haste to fill the cup, then fussed about drying the mess with a towel while Father Gallagher held the cup to Sister Joan's lips. After a few sips, she could take a deep breath.

"I'm all right," she said shakily. "I just never expected... I never thought..."

Sister Martina blotted at the papers on her desk helplessly, while glancing at her superiors, her expression very clearly wondering what strange news Father Gallagher must have brought to make Sister Joan Phillippe wilt like that.

"That will be all, Sister Martina." Sister Joan Phillippe waved her hand weakly in dismissal. "Father Gallagher and I need to confer in private for a time. Please close the door on your way out."

Father Gallagher's eyebrows rose. "Maybe Sister Martina should bring us some tea first. You still look a bit shaky."

"I'm fine, Father Gallagher. That won't be necessary." Sister Joan Phillippe waited until the little nun had departed and softly closed the door. Then she opened the bottom drawer of her desk and withdrew a bottle of cherry wine and two glasses. Father Gallagher's eyes widened and he smothered full-out laughter.

"I never would have believed it, Sister," he managed to say with a straight face, after biting off a grin that tried desperately to break out of his normally stern face.

"It's good for treating hysteria," she said primly. "One of the first things you learn when you live with a bunch of women day in and day out. Sooner or later, everyone has one of 'those' days. A small glass of wine can ease the nerves as long as it does not become a habit. And I see that it does not become a habit with any of my nuns." The look she gave him served well to smother levity in any form among her staff.

"I'm sure you do," Father Gallagher said, watching her pour generous glasses of the precious wine. "But might I say, that's slightly more than a small glass you're serving there."

She sighed deeply. "I'm afraid this story is going to be harder than most of my counseling sessions. Michael, I need to hear what you've been told. Then I'm going to have to tell you a story of my own. It's one I had hoped I would never have to revisit again. I'm afraid we're both going to need this."

~~~~~

Taking her glass of wine, she moved over to the softer chairs by the fireplace in the corner of the room and settled in, motioning for Father Gallagher to join her. Taking a sip of the sweet wine, he followed her and settled into the second chair. It was not lost on him that she had reverted to using his Christian name. So, they were back on more familiar turf than their usual formalities.

Interesting… He took a sip of wine and swallowed.

"This… man—for lack of a better word—has been spotted in the woods, but he has avoided the company of other men so far. A few homes along the outskirts have reported petty thievery, such as missing loaves of bread or vegetables. Not enough to hurt their families or cause them hardship, but enough to be noticeable. Usually, these occasions of missing food occur right about the time this 'man' has been seen in the area." Father Gallagher watched her closely as he spoke and saw her jaw tighten, the lines around her eyes deepening. He was confirming something with every word he spoke, and he could see it written on her face. "He hasn't hurt anyone, but evidently there was a sailor in port this week from Cherbourg. When he heard the rumors, he is said to have gone positively gray." Father Gallagher paused. "Almost the same reaction you had, Sister."

"Indeed," Sister Joan Phillippe muttered, staring into the flames of the fireplace. She took another sip of wine. "Proceed, Michael."

"He told an interesting tale of a man who had been stitched together by a mad scientist late in the last century. Of course, the rest of the men in the inn scoffed at the tale, but those who had come in from the country weren't laughing. They said the scars could well have been left by a surgeon's stitches, though they didn't get close enough for examination. The sailor said he was a murderous monster who had killed the man who made him, as well as everyone else associated with that man—women and children included. He said one look in his dark eyes was enough to make your blood run cold, but that he seemed to be impervious to bullets. He wasn't sure what could kill the monster short of dismembering it the same way it had been put together, but no one had been able to subdue it long enough to attempt such a feat."

Father Gallagher's frown deepened as he watched tears gather in Sister Joan Phillippe's eyes and trickle down her cheeks. Were those wrinkles? He'd never noticed before, but the good Sister was beginning to
~~~~~

show signs of aging. She had not been a young woman when he'd first come to her convent in France as a lad of ten, and that had been over thirty years ago. And yet, he hated to think of her growing old and dying on him. He realized with a pang that that was exactly what would happen one day. But for now—something about this story bothered her.

"Is that all?" she whispered, when he had been silent for several moments.

Father Gallagher blinked. He had lost his train of thought.

"Would you like to tell me your story now, Sister?" he asked softly. "It sounds like it might be a burden more easily borne if it's shared. Don't you think so?"

"I never wanted to… to lay this upon anyone else," she replied. "It was so long ago. I had hoped… But alas, look at me. I never thought I'd live so long and he… was created to endure. Why should he not still survive? I laid it before the Lord so many years ago, and I trusted that He would deal with the individuals… But it seems that we are going to be called upon to be His hands and feet even in this."

Father Gallagher waited while she took another sip of wine and leaned back against her chair. She stared into the fire and he saw her memories unfold as her words came tumbling forth, halting at first, and then in a torrent, as flood waters released.

~~~~~

I had been with the Sisters of the Maid for a mere seven years when these things I must speak of happened. They had received me with open arms after my own attack, and I had learned much about battling the evil forces in this world. Somehow vampires always seemed to find our little corner of the world, but God gave us the strength to defeat them.

Sister Daniella opened our gate one morning and found a huge man lying in the road just outside. She called to me and I ran to help her. I immediately noted the grayness of his skin, and we thought he had been attacked by a vampire. But it was so much worse. He was covered in old burns, long untreated, and stab wounds that had festered and putrefied. The nuns even removed several lead balls from his torso when they treated him. Proof he had been shot with a pistol. I soon noticed the stitches around his neck and wrists. Later, we were to find them around his ankles and elsewhere on his body. He looked like a poorly sewn patchwork quilt. He also had metal bolts in his neck. I couldn't figure that part out. Why would anyone put metal bolts in a man's neck? It took four of us to get him on his feet and walking. He was barely able to shuffle into the convent. We put him in our quarantine room, which was—
~~~~~

thankfully!—empty at the time.

For three days, we nursed him through a fever. His constitution was amazing. He was weakened, but with nourishing food and rest, he regained his strength faster than I could have ever imagined. But he eyed us with suspicion every day. His answers were curt, even rude, most of the time. He grudgingly thanked us for the meals we gave him, and once his strength began to return, he refused to allow us to tend to his scars. We tried rubbing aromatic oils and herbs into the scars, but he rebuffed us at every turn. He cared nothing for the aesthetics of his deformities.

On the fourth day, I brought the man his breakfast, a bowl of hearty cooked oats with honey and berries. But he wasn't lying in bed. I gasped in surprise and gripped the wooden tray tightly to keep from dropping his meal on the floor. We knew he was a large man, of course, but seeing him standing upright and without fever, his eyes fearsome and dark— well, it was a frightening moment.

He was well over seven and a half feet tall, taller than any man I'd ever seen in my life. His shoulders were broad and his arms were thickly corded bands of muscles, ending in clenched fists. His legs braced his body below the nightshirt we had hastily fashioned for him out of sheets that first night, sewn by candlelight while the nuns in the infirmary tried to dress the worst of his wounds and bring down his fever.

"Where am I? And why am I a prisoner here?" he asked. His voice was raspy, but filled with such malice, I cringed.

"You are no prisoner, sir," I said. "You are our guest. This is a convent. We are the Sisters of the Maid, a holy order dedicated to serving people. You needed help, so we tended your wounds and treated your fever." I spoke gently, but his eyes narrowed. He did not trust me, and I dared not move from my place by the door lest he mistake my motives for coming closer.

"No one 'helps' me without another reason," he scoffed contemptuously. "Who have you told about my presence here?"

I frowned a bit at that. Was he a criminal? Hiding from the authorities? Wanted for crimes in the cities perhaps? But our vows were not to the laws of this earth. They were to God. I wondered if I had skills enough to convince him of this. *Help me, O Lord, and give me Your wisdom and Your words.* I could only hope that quick prayer would be enough!

"No one has been told, sir," I said softly. "We have simply cared for you because you were in need. It's what we do."

"**Why?**" he asked, taking a step closer. "Why did you do this for me? Looking the way I do. Why did you bother to help me?"

I forced myself not to take a step backward, even though every particle of my being told me to throw that tray at him and run. "B-b-because it is what God commands of us. We have taken vows to serve God with our every breath. This is the path we have chosen. We serve the people who come to us in need. Y-you were most definitely in need."

He stared at me for an eternity and I dared not look away from those dark, dreadful eyes. I met his gaze with all the sincerity I could muster, somehow knowing that my life, and possibly everyone else's as well, hung in the balance. He finally took a step back, wobbled slightly, then sat on the edge of the bed. It sagged under his weight. He dropped his head into both hands.

"I don't understand you," he said. "But I am obviously not able to travel yet. So tell me, woman who serves this God, am I going to be safe here? Or am I going to have to fight off a bunch of villagers with pitchforks? Because I warn you now, if it comes to such a battle, I will not be the loser in the end. You've evidently seen my scars, so you know I've battled many enemies. Most of them did not survive the encounter."

My fear and, yes, a certain revulsion must have shown on my face. He was a murderer! And here he sat almost bragging about his conquests.

His anger flared and he shot to his feet. This time I did take a step backward in alarm.

"I have never taken a life except to defend my own," he cried. Then he paused and sagged. "No, that's not true. There was one... no, two... but the first was an accident..." He stopped and shook his head. "Why am I telling you this? You have no idea what my life has been like! No idea what they have done to me — what *he* did to me. I wanted to be gentle and kind. I tried. But... your world has no place for the likes of me."

His anguish touched my heart, in spite of my fear, and I gripped the tray in my hands more lightly.

"Sir, you need sustenance. Please eat now. Sister Francisca is a very fine cook, and she made you these oats this morning, with honey from our beehives and fresh berries picked just this morning."

"You've poisoned it, haven't you?" His voice was flat.

"What?" I was taken aback by the very suggestion. "Of course not!"

"Then you eat it."

"But I have had breakfast, and you are the one who must eat to regain your strength."

"I don't believe you," he said, standing over me. He wrenched the tray forcefully from my hands. "Take the spoon and eat a bite of this."

I sighed as I took up the spoon. "No one is trying to hurt you. We mean you no harm at all, I promise you before God." I ate some of the oatmeal carefully so he could clearly see me spoon it into my mouth and swallow.

His eyes narrowed. "You didn't eat a berry with that bite. Are the berries poisonous?"

I sighed more deeply this time. "No, the berries are absolutely delicious, so I was trying to save them for you. But if you insist..." I scooped up another spoonful and made sure to catch a fat blackberry this time. I couldn't help smiling just a little as I bit into the sweet fruit. Blackberries were a special favorite of mine. I set the spoon back on the tray and stared at the giant glaring down at me.

"See? I'm fine. You have nothing to fear from us. We are not trying to harm you in any way. Now will you eat your breakfast before it gets cold?"

He grunted, still watching me for signs of illness, but he sat with the tray on his lap and took a tentative bite. Soon he was shoveling in the tasty oats almost faster than he could swallow. I turned to leave the room and he stopped me with muffled "mmmfff..." I waited until he had swallowed the mouthful.

He stared for a moment longer, then mumbled, "Thank you."

I smiled. It was a start. "You're welcome. I'll be back with some fresh water from the well. And if you want more, I might be able to refill that bowl if you want me to."

We developed a rapport, the strange giant and I. I maintained a healthy distance and a respectful attitude. But with the infirmary nuns, he became downright surly. He refused to allow them to change his bandages once he was on his feet again. He demanded his own clothes back. Sister Katherine was a marvel with needle and thread. She had already noted the terrible condition of the clothes he came in wearing. When they'd been stripped off of him and washed thoroughly, she had used them as guidelines to cut new clothes from the cloth we wove ourselves. She dyed some of it with dark walnut to stain it brown, figuring correctly that he would not want to be clothed like a nun! The shirt material she left white. She'd worked tirelessly to finish the first pair of pants and shirt while he still lay with the fever, believing firmly that he would survive. So, when I had to tell him that the clothes he had worn into the convent had all but fallen apart when we washed them, I was relieved to be able to present him with the clothes she had just finished making.

"Someone made these for me?" he asked. "Why would she do that?"

"Because you needed clothes," I said. "And we knew we could not buy them for you. No one would be making clothes big enough to fit someone your size. Besides, you seemed most anxious that no one outside our community know about your presence here. So Sister Katherine made them herself."

"Is there anyone else in the convent besides you nuns?" he asked.

"Not usually, though we do receive deliveries from the village twice a week for meat and flour, milk and cheese. We barter with honey and the fruits and vegetables from our gardens, and sometimes other things we make by hand. Why?"

"I-I would like to help around here. Perhaps chop some wood, or work in the fields, but I don't want to be seen by others. Is that possible?"

I considered that. He was actually offering to help us with manual labor? He was not at all what I expected from someone who had admittedly killed people.

"I'll talk to Mother Superior about that, but for now, perhaps you should try to rest first."

"I've rested enough." He waved an impatient hand at me.

"May I ask you…?" I began hesitantly.

He glared at me, daring me to say the wrong thing.

"What is your name?"

He stared for a moment, clearly startled by the question. I wondered what he had thought I was going to ask, and was glad I had avoided whatever it was. He turned away and stared out the window, his Adam's apple bobbing convulsively.

"I don't have a name," he whispered.

I frowned. "Have you suffered a memory loss?"

"No!" he snapped. Then he softened his tone. "No, my father never gave me a name. He made me, then he cast me out. He was afraid of me, ashamed of me. He—he never bothered to give me a name."

"I'm sorry," I said gently. "I didn't mean to pry. I just wanted to be able to address you by a name instead of always saying 'sir'. But I didn't mean to anger you."

I turned to go, but he stopped me. "Wh-what's your name?"

I paused. "My name is Sister Joan Phillippe."

"Really?" I saw the first hint of a smile cross his lips. "Such a big name for so little a nun. You have three names and I am left with nothing but the label of 'monster'." His smile became a grimace.

"Then perhaps we should give you a name," I said impulsively. "What name do you like?"

"That's usually the father's job, isn't it?" he asked grimly. "Naming the son is supposed to be his duty."

"Some boys lose their fathers to death, war, disease. Some lose their mothers. We cannot always follow the threads that make up the tapestry of our lives. But we can make the most of the opportunities we are given. And here is your opportunity right now to have a name of your own. You say it, and we will make it official."

"What do you mean 'official'?" he asked with a frown.

"I'll have to talk to Mother Superior," I said, afraid I might have overstepped myself. "Usually babies are brought to us, presented to God and named. But in your case, perhaps, we could allow you to come to the chapel and sort of present yourself. We could have a little ceremony and make your name known to God by prayer. Truly, He already knows who you are. We are just letting Him know that you know He has led you here, and He has preserved your life thus far."

"*God* has preserved me?" the giant exploded. "I don't think so, Sister Joan Phillippe of the long name. *I* have preserved myself with my own hands! And it has not been easy, thanks to humans. I've had to struggle and fight for every scrap of food and every breath of air."

I stood frozen as his rage filled the room. He saw the look on my face, and he retreated into his shell again. I fled the room.

<div align="center">~~~~~</div>

Sister Mary Agatha was the ample-figured infirmary nun, and she was ready to wash her hands of our 'guest'. Over tea with her and Mother Superior, I confessed that I had blundered with him that morning and enraged him to such a point, I had fled in fear.

"You said nothing wrong, child," Mother Superior assured me. "It was a lovely idea. Though I would really like to know more about this man he calls 'father'. It does not sound like a father-son relationship as we understand one. That troubles me. Perhaps our guest will change his mind later. You have planted the seed in his heart, and now you must trust the Holy Spirit to water and nurture that seed until it grows."

"Well, he refuses to allow me to change his bandages, and he has even refused my nightly infusions. I reassured him that they are only to help him sleep more peacefully." Plump Sister Mary Agatha reminded me of one of our hens who always seemed to have ruffled feathers and a perpetually grumpy disposition. "Would you believe he wanted me to take it first? I told him I couldn't take it. I had to be up all night in case other patients needed me. I might sleep right on through their cries for help if I took that medicine."

I tried to stifle a giggle, but I wasn't very successful.

121

"He said, 'I knew it! You want to poison me.' Me!" she continued. "An infirmary care giver! I would never poison a living soul! Why, the nerve of that man!"

Mother Superior observed her for a moment. "Perhaps we could slip some of your medicines into his meals, Sister Mary Agatha. Do you think he'd notice the taste?"

My giggles broke through then. "Oh no! Please don't, Mother Superior!" She looked at me in surprise. "You see, he makes me taste everything I bring him from the kitchen. If you put something in his food, you'll be picking me up off the floor, and he'll know for sure what you've done."

"Oh dear." She paled a bit. "Sister Joan Phillippe, that's not funny! Not in the slightest. You should have told me at once that this was going on."

I sobered at once, my laughter trailing off.

Sister Mary Agatha looked a bit green around the gills too. "Oh, my… what if…" She crossed herself rapidly and picked at the rosary beads on her belt. "Mother, I had no idea."

"We were adding some herbs to some of his food," Mother Superior said softly, coming to sit with me as she took my hands in hers. "They were strictly to build his strength up, so there was nothing that could have hurt you."

I grew cold at the possibilities of what she was saying.

"But if we had moved on to other medications, who knows what might have happened? From now on, I want a daily report on all your interactions with our guest. No more surprises. Yes?"

I nodded. She released my hands and pressed my teacup into them. The cup trembled slightly, and she patted my forearm.

"Drink, child. It will help."

Obediently I did as she directed, but I still felt the chill in my heart.

"His temper…" I whispered.

"Yes, that is a concern." Mother Superior nodded. "Had he realized what we were doing, he might have attacked us all, thinking we meant him harm. No more herbs. Allow his body to heal on its own. If he needs help, we will have to trust that he will ask for it. Or that somehow God Himself will give us the grace with this man that he will trust us to care for him again. If not… well, perhaps that is God's will instead."

I gasped. "Mother! You can't mean we would let him die!"

"If he will not let us help him, we might have to, my daughter." Her voice was filled with sorrow. "It is not what I want, but I cannot risk the lives of everyone under this roof if he is that mistrustful of us. He has been here for six days now, and still, he thinks we mean to harm him? Something—or someone—has damaged his mind to a terrible extent. God forgive me, but I will not sacrifice fifteen servants of God for one … I don't even know if he's truly a man or not!"

I remembered something he'd said. How had he phrased it? I felt my forehead pucker as I tried to remember his exact words. Mother Superior noticed.

"What is it, Sister Joan Phillippe?"

"Something he said," I mumbled. "I want to recall his exact words. They were so strange." Both nuns waited for me. "'I have preserved myself with my own hands! And it has not been easy, thanks to humans.'" I paused. "That was what he said. It was like he didn't consider himself in the same category as the rest of us. But what can that mean?"

We didn't know, but we were troubled by those words, and they would come back to haunt me over and over.

~~~~~

For two more days, the man ate in silence. I brought his meals and he would stare at me until I took a bite of each portion of food. Then he would accept the tray and I would leave him to eat with only a nod. On the third day, he ventured out of his room and wandered around the garden. Seeing him, I managed to maneuver toward him, picking weeds as I made my way along the row of green beans. When I was within conversational distance, I spoke softly.

"If you hear the bell at the gate, you will want to go inside. It means someone from the village is requesting entry," I said.

I glanced up and saw him nod once, then he moved away, keeping close to the wall, his head ducked down as though hiding his face from God, from us.

Later that afternoon, we heard the ringing of an axe, and I knew that he had found the wood pile behind the kitchen. Sister Mary Agatha had just mentioned at luncheon that she was going to have to take the time to gather kindling and chop some wood or we would be serving cold meals within the next couple of days. It was not her favorite chore. I peeked around the corner of the building, and there was our guest, wielding the axe like it was a child's toy, and splitting logs with one stroke that would have taken any of us several tries to break apart. There was still a degree of rage in his movements, but it was controlled, constructive. And very welcome to us.

That night, I spied the man sitting in the far back corner of the chapel
~~~~~

as we said our evening devotions and sang our praises to the Lord. He kept looking at the wooden cross over our simple altar, then his head would lower and I could see nothing but the long, dark hair that hid his face from the world. As we filed out after our service had ended, I noticed Mother Superior had approached him and offered him a Bible. He tried to push it away and brush past her, but something she said stopped him. He turned back to her slowly, head still bowed. Then he nodded, and allowed her to slip the book into his massive hands. He nodded again, and I heard her say, "…day or night… I am here if you need to talk…" Then we were out of the building and headed for our rooms for the night. Three a.m. prayers came very early, and we were ready to retire after evening prayers, but I was curious about the exchange I had seen and wondered what seeds our wise Mother Superior was planting!

During the next week, I would see the man sitting under a tree, reading from the Bible Mother Superior had given him. Sometimes frowning, but often with a thoughtful look upon his face. When the Book was open to the middle, which meant the Psalms, I would sometimes see a peaceful look come over him, but often it was a tearful look of wonder, as though King David had tapped into the man's torment as much as his own. In those few moments, I felt a miracle might be just around the corner, but then some little thing would set him off, and his temper would ignite a veritable battle in the infirmary!

Sister Mary Agatha noticed a blister on his hand from the old axe handle, and a huge splinter protruding from the midst of it.

"That could fester and putrefy if you don't let me cleanse it," she protested when he pushed her bodily from the room.

"My whole body is a putrefaction! Don't you understand that?" he roared.

"No! I don't!" she yelled back. "Because it isn't. I treated your body for two whole days and I saw wounds and scars that needed tending, but you are not putrefying, young man!"

He stopped and stared at her. "That can't be. You don't know what you're talking about! Leave me **alone**!"

She backed out of his room as he glowered at her menacingly. "I do know what I'm talking about. Whoever told you you're dying inside was wrong." Tears stung her eyes. "We've never lied to you. Not once. All we've done is try to help you. You're only damaging yourself now." She turned and stalked away.

I witnessed this episode from the doorway with his dinner tray in my hands. Slowly, I set the tray on the small bedside table. Sister Mary

Agatha's metal bowl, which she filled with water and used for tending wounds, had been tossed in the corner, and water was dashed across the floor along with her rags. He picked up his spoon and began to eat without making me taste it this time. I held in my surprise, and knelt to retrieve the rags and sop up the water.

"You don't have to do that," he said gruffly.

"Someone could slip and fall," I replied softly. "Best to clean it up. I won't be long, and I promise not to disturb you while you eat." I made quick work of the floor and retrieved the bowl. When I looked up, he was still watching me while he chewed. But his eyes were thoughtful instead of stormy.

"Could I see your hand?" I asked timidly.

Impatience creased his forehead, but he thrust his right hand toward me. There was indeed a sizeable pocket of pus with a blister below it. And in the middle of the pus was a splinter of wood.

"That old axe has left pieces of itself imbedded in all of us at one time or another," I admitted ruefully. "Would you allow me to clean that out and remove the splinter after you've finished eating? If I was very careful?"

"Why?" he asked.

"Because it must hurt. Because it could worsen and bring back your fever. Because I want to help you. Because you are wounded and it is the mission given to us to heal wounds here, not to inflict them. You got this doing us a service. We would not want you to be hurt trying to help us. Are those enough reasons?"

"I don't understand you people." He shook his head. "I've never met anyone like you before." He stared at me for several moments, then he finally nodded his assent.

I went to draw clean water and to gather fresh linens. Then I spoke to Sister Mary Agatha to ask if there was anything in particular I should do about the splinter. She gave me the small pliers she kept in a pouch on her belt.

"There is so much pus in the wound, it should slide right out," she muttered. "But be careful that he doesn't take a swing at you. It may hurt. Try to get anything yellow or green-tinged out of the wound, then wrap it in clean cloth with this ointment." She hugged me briefly and made the sign of the cross over my forehead. "Protect her, Lord Jesus."

The man watched me while I worked on his hand. I felt his gaze, even when I didn't look up. He never flinched or cried out, even when I pulled the splinter out, and it turned out to be much larger than we had thought.

It had been imbedded deep into his palm. I marveled at his tolerance for pain, even as I winced in sympathy. When I had finally finished cleaning the last of the pus from his palm and was wrapping his hand tenderly in the clean linens, he spoke.

"I have decided on a name," he said.

That conversation had been more than a fortnight ago! Yet he was picking it up as if we had discussed it only yesterday.

"And what have you chosen? May I know it?" I asked with a smile.

"Well, I wondered if you would let me have one of your names, since you have so many." He watched my face as he said it, gauging my response.

"You … want to be called —?"

"Phillippe."

"Really?"

"What does it mean?"

"Actually, it means 'one who loves horses'," I said with a chuckle.

The man smiled! "One who loves horses? And how did you come up with that?"

I sighed. "When I came here, I, too, was wounded. In my heart and soul, I had been wounded by those I expected to stand by me forever. Here with these sisters, I found my faith again, and I found a home and a purpose. I took the name 'Joan' for our founding saint, Joan de Arc. She was a great warrior many years ago. I took the name Phillippe for the monk who had saved my life back in England. He vanquished an evil monster and saved me from it, then he taught me how to protect myself in case I should meet others like that one in the future."

"And did you?" he asked, his eyes narrowed. "Meet other monsters?"

"Yes, I have," I responded softly. "Many of them. This is an order that fights the monsters that threaten the innocent people in our world."

"Yet you took me in. And you continue to help me. Why?"

"Because you are not a monster. You are just a wounded man who needs the Lord, just as we all do."

"You do not know me. You don't understand." His voice broke, and a tear trickled down his leathery cheek.

"You can tell me and I will try to understand," I said, taking his huge hand in my small ones. "I do want to help you if I can. We all do. You have kindness in you, and we see it. But something holds you back. Whatever it is that you fear, I believe we can help you find your way. I know God can help you."

"God has turned His back on me," the man said sadly.

"If God had turned His back on you, He would not have led you to us," I said firmly.

His head came up and he stared directly into my eyes. "You really believe that, don't you?"

I nodded.

He slowly stood and looked out the window for several moments. When he turned to me again, his eyes held a new resolve. "I will think about what you have said, Sister Joan Phillippe."

For several days, he kept his distance, took his meals in silence. He nodded his thanks, but he no longer required that I taste his meals. I was heartened, but still cautious around him. I noticed his huge frame slipping into the shadows when we said our prayers together at night and in the wee hours of the morning, and there were baskets of potatoes and turnips from the fields by the kitchen door on the tenth morning.

"The ground is so hard," marveled Sister Francesca, our cook. "He must have worked all night to harvest so much of our crop at one time." She genuflected. "May the Lord bless him for his kindness."

Mother Superior had joined us by the door. "I don't think it's kindness that drives him, Sister Francesca, but we can be grateful for his gift to us nonetheless." She motioned for me to follow her. "I want you to give him this, Sister Joan Phillippe," she said pressing a prayer book into my hands. "You may tell him how much we appreciate the things he has been doing for us, and that we wish him to have it." She sighed and a pucker appeared between her eyebrows. "Perhaps it will bring him a measure of peace. I had hoped..." Her voice trailed off.

"You thought he would come to you for counsel, didn't you?" I said softly.

She nodded slowly. "But for some men, it is hard to seek help from a mere woman. Yes? Even when the woman is a nun."

I smiled sadly. Some things would likely never change. And Mother Superior was correct. His heart was very troubled. Maybe a prayer book would help him as I knew it had helped me over the last seven years.

I found him sitting under a tree with his head in his hands. He looked up as I approached, watching warily as I sank to my knees in the soft grass.

"I have a gift for you from Mother Superior," I said. "We are so grateful for the food you left by the kitchen this morning. That was a very generous thing you did."

He shrugged off my comment and looked away. "I don't need gifts. You've fed and clothed me. So I helped you." I saw him swallow hard. "It was nothing."

"It meant a great deal to us. We would have worked for several days to gather that much. Can we not express our gratitude to you? Will you not allow that?" I kept my tone soft, and smiled gently, hoping to soften the giant man's heart.

He looked at my hands and saw the book. I held it out to him, hoping he would take it, praying his curiosity would get the better of him.

It did.

"What is this?"

"It's a prayer book," I said. "We use books like this for our prayer times with God. Sometimes it helps when you don't know what to pray, or you can't find the words your heart wants to say. And sometimes it just helps to know that others have felt the same pain and frustrations that you feel yourself at a given moment. When bitterness overwhelms you, there are prayers to help you take that pain to God and leave it at His feet—"

"Bitterness?" he cut me off sharply. "What would you know about bitterness, Sister Joan Phillippe? What would you know about pain and rejection?"

"Actually, I'm well acquainted with them," I said when his angry outburst died down. He looked at me sharply.

"How could someone like you know of the bitterness I've felt? The rejection from the one who was supposed to love you? The total denial of every desire, every dream of a future you saw before you? You know nothing," he spat.

"I suffered all of that and more," I said, tears forming in my eyes. "I suffered being called a liar by the very people I looked up to, the people who had vowed before God to cherish me and guide me for the entirety of my life. I lost everything. I was cast out! I couldn't go home because my family called me crazy, I—" A sob wrenched from my throat and I forced myself to take a deep, shaky breath.

"Will you tell me?" His voice was strangely soft. I looked into those dark eyes and suddenly knew that I had to share my story. I didn't want to. I didn't want to open myself up that much to this strange man. But I knew that the condition of his very soul might depend on what I said next.

"I was a young nun, being sent on my first mission with four other sisters and a priest to Ireland. Along the way, we were joined by three monks who shared the road with us. It was a dangerous trip, and there was a little more safety in numbers. Oh, how grateful I am to God for those monks!

"When Sister Caroleen sickened and died at the end of our first week,

I was given the task of preparing her body for burial. Sister Angeline took the bucket to the spring for clean water while I undressed her, and that was when I noticed the marks on Sister Caroleen's neck. Two small puncture wounds. I was so intent upon examining these strange wounds, I didn't hear the priest sneak up behind me until he had attacked and bitten me. One of the monks was nearby, expecting such an attack, as I later learned, and he leapt forward and plunged a wooden stake through the priest's heart. The priest disappeared, vanishing into a pile of ash. The monk had encountered vampires in his home village before entering the brotherhood, and he had recognized the signs when Sister Caroleen became sick. His own sister had perished in similar fashion when he was a boy."

"What is a vampire?" He frowned, for the word obviously held no meaning to him.

"Nosferatu, the undead," I said, "A vampire is one who is cursed. They have died, but they live again and walk the earth. But to continue to 'live', they must consume the blood of the living, and in so doing, they drain the life from those people, and when they die, they become vampires as well. They are pure evil; they destroy for destruction's sake, and they take pleasure in that destruction. They hate the things of God, and it is by those very things—the cross, and holy water, for example—that we are able to fight them and protect the innocent."

"So, you were bitten, but you did not become this evil thing yourself?" he asked.

"No, I did not die," I explained, twisting my rosary beads in my hands. This was the hard part to relive. I took a deep breath. "We finished our journey together. Brother Phillippe treated my wounds with holy water, and the brothers and Sister Angeline prayed with me constantly. I ran a slight fever, and felt some weakness, but I recovered quickly since the priest was no longer alive to continue feeding on me. When we reached the monastery, we were questioned about the absence of the priest and Sister Caroleen." I paused, my voice catching as a tear slid down my cheek. "They didn't believe us. They separated us, questioned us endlessly, then the questions became harsh. I was thought to be insane."

Tears fell more freely as the pain returned. I had been staring at the beads in my lap as I told the first part of my story, but at that point, I raised my gaze to his face. His expression told me he was hanging on every word.

"The others eventually recanted under the torture they endured at the hands of those we had trusted with our very souls. They thought we had been deceived, you see. Or rather, that the others had been deceived by me. They thought they were acting for our own good. But I knew what had happened to me, and I would not say what was not true just to placate them. So, they cast me out of the church. I tried to go home, but my father turned me out as well. The church had deemed me crazy, and my family disowned and disavowed me. I ran until I could run no further. I ran to the coast and stowed away aboard the first vessel I found. When it landed, I slipped ashore and I ran again. I collapsed, just as you did, right outside that gate." I pointed to the large wooden gate across the field. His gaze left mine for only a moment to follow my finger.

"The Sisters brought me in, treated my wounds, which were many, cared for me, fed me, and allowed me to heal here." I swallowed hard. "Then one day a woman was brought to the infirmary with the same wounds on her neck. I became hysterical. 'I know what did this!' I screamed. 'It was a monster! You must believe me! It was a vampire! It will attack her again.' Mother Superior took me aside and said very simply, 'We know.' I was stunned. She told me they knew what to do, how to deal with it, and they would protect the woman as they would protect me. I wanted to know how."

"Did they teach you?"

I smiled as I nodded. "Oh, yes. I learned how to destroy vampires, how to protect the innocent, how to heal the wounded, and I learned that no pit is so deep that God cannot reach down and rescue the one who has fallen and cannot get out by himself. Even the pits of despair that we dig for ourselves."

I felt his thumb gently reach over and brush the tears from my cheeks, one at a time.

"Thank you for telling me this, Sister Joan Phillippe. I know it was not easy—"

The bell rang out, announcing a visitor, and I saw Sister Daniella hurrying to respond to the summons. My companion jumped to his feet and looked for some place to duck out of sight, but the gate was swinging open. He spun to hide behind the tree, but it could not disguise his massive size. I tried to stand in front of the part of him that still was visible, but knew it was a futile gesture.

Francois from the dairy in town shaded his eyes and frowned as he peered in our direction. He pointed and tugged at Sister Daniella. She realized her mistake at once and tried to tell him it was just a traveler, but I could see that he did not believe her explanation. He turned and ran. Even from that distance, I could hear his cries, and my blood ran cold.

"Monster! Monster in the abbey!"

"I must leave this place," he said softly.

"I'm so sorry," I said, placing my hands on his massive arm. Sister Daniella and Mother Superior both hastened in our direction. Sister Daniella burbled her apologies, tripping over her words and crying tears of remorse for not looking about for him before she opened the gate. It was all her fault.

"Make sure to take your bag, and the books we've given you," Mother Superior said. "You are going with our many thanks for all your hard work on our behalf and our constant prayers for your safety."

"And you go with my name," I said, pressing his arm. "Phillippe you are from this day forward, even though we did not have a chance to make it official. God knows you. That's all that is important."

Sister Agatha came running with his pack. "I threw everything in it when I heard Francois running away. Your Bible is in there too. Go before they return."

"Go… Phillippe," Mother Superior said, making the sign of the cross before him with her hand. "Go with our every blessing, my son."

Tears gathered in his eyes as he turned and fled across the fields. He would break through the fence on the far side of the abbey grounds, then fill it back in with stones before striking out across France.

We never saw him again.

~~~~~

Sister Joan Phillippe sipped the last of her wine and stared into the flames. Father Gallagher gazed into the flames as though he'd been spellbound as she told her story. He shook his head when she stopped speaking.

"What did the villagers do?"

She leaned her head against the tall chair and sighed. "They were furious. And fearful, of course. They demanded to be allowed to search the premises. Mother Superior permitted it, because to deny them access would have endangered everyone under our roof. She only allowed two men to come into the infirmary though, two who were the calmest and least likely to frighten our patients. Of course, they found nothing except an extra-large bed in one room. Mother Superior explained that we had treated a traveler for his injuries, then he had departed when he was well enough to travel, and that it was our duty before God to treat anyone who came to our door seeking shelter and aid, was it not? They had no answer for that, other than the obvious one."

A soft tap on the door caused her to grimace.
~~~~~

"I told her no interruptions," she grumbled. "Come," she said more loudly.

The door swung inward and a massive form filled the entryway.

Sister Joan Phillippe gasped and rose from her seat, one hand automatically reaching for her rosary.

"Phillippe!"

The figure smiled. "Sister Joan Phillippe of the long name. You remembered me."

Father Gallagher rose and stared at their visitor. His gaze darted from Sister Joan Phillippe to the stranger and back again, and suddenly Sister Joan Phillippe saw his face relax as he forced his features into a smile.

"I'm Father Gallagher, and I believe we were just talking about you, sir."

Phillippe's eyebrows rose and a hint of a smile played at his lips. "Really? Why, Sister Joan Phillippe! I didn't expect you to go telling monster stories."

She frowned reprovingly. "You are not a monster, Phillippe. You never were. And we just heard rumor today that you might be in the area. That's the only reason I related your story to Father Gallagher. It's the first time I've ever told that story, in fact. So might I ask, what on earth has brought you to my door after all these years?" She stepped forward and embraced the giant man, much to his surprise. He stepped inside and closed the door.

"I have news of a most serious nature, Sister. I had to risk coming here. I believe you are in danger."

Father Gallagher suppressed a laugh. "When are we not in danger, my friend? We hunt and destroy vampires. I'm sorry, but danger is a very real part of our lives on a daily basis."

Phillippe stepped further into the room. "This is more. This goes deeper than you know. Have you ever heard of—"

The door slammed open and Abraham Van Helsing burst into the room, pistol drawn. "Back! Stand back!"

Sister Joan Phillippe threw herself in front of Phillippe and shrieked, "**No!** Abraham, no! Do not shoot him! He is a friend."

Dr. Van Helsing straightened abruptly and raised the pistol to point at the ceiling. "*Vas ist das*? A friend, you say?"

"Yes," she sighed. "A dear old friend. We are in no danger from him, and he says he has news for us. Please put the pistol away. Phillippe, this is Dr. Abraham Van Helsing."

"Van Helsing," he said, eyeing the newcomer with interest. "I have heard your name in Europe. The vampires have no love for you, that is certain."

"Ha! That is good to know!" Van Helsing said with a light of approval in his blue eyes.

"The news, Phillippe?" Sister Joan Phillippe asked, turning once again to the giant.

"Have you heard of a man named Arnold Paole?" They all shook their heads negatively. Phillippe sighed. "He lived in the last century in Austria, dying of a broken neck. But he claimed to have eaten the earth from the grave of a vampire and smeared himself with the vampire's blood as a cure from the Turkish vampire who had been tormenting him. Evidently his little home remedy didn't work. Villagers reported being visited by Arnold well after his death and burial, then they began dying off at an alarming rate. Supposedly they dug him up, drove a stake through his heart and burned the body. But they must have lied because he's very much alive and well. Or undead and well, I guess you would say."

"You've seen him?" Sister Joan Phillippe asked. "You've confirmed this?"

"Oh, yes," he said grimly. "From his top hat and spectacles down to his shiny shoes."

"What is that?" Van Helsing's head snapped up. "His top hat, you said?"

"He favors a fancy top hat and a silk scarf. He has become something of a dandy over the past century." Phillippe snorted derisively.

Father Gallagher paled. "Top hat!"

Phillippe frowned as he watched their reactions grow. "This means something to you."

"Yes," Van Helsing said, stroking his chin thoughtfully. "We have a close friend. One who shares the work we do. She has been watched by this creature. Watched far too closely. Until now, we had no clue about his identity. But why? That is still the question."

"Perhaps I can answer it," Phillippe said carefully. "You see Arnold Paole is not the man calling the shots. Have you ever heard of a priest called Hunderprest?"

Sister Joan Phillippe's legs folded and Phillippe caught her before she hit the floor. Van Helsing shoved a chair behind her knees and Father Gallagher poured a little more wine into her glass, then pressed it to her lips.

"Drink, Sister," he urged.

"That name means something to you," Phillippe stated when her color returned to normal.

"Th-that's ancient church history," she protested. "Surely not…"

Father Gallagher stared at her a moment, then back at Phillippe. "Not the zombie priest of Melrose Abbey! But that's a myth!"

"Is it?" Phillippe's mouth twisted. "And what is my own story but a piece of fiction, penned by a young girl not yet twenty?"

"Enlighten an ignorant old man, if you please," Van Helsing said with a bow.

"In the spring of 1196, Hunderprest died in Scotland," Phillippe said. "He was not a very nice man during his life, and I doubt that his passing was lamented. He left several mistresses dotting the countryside, and seemed to prefer hunting with his dogs to doing his spiritual duties. He was known for his cruelty, even to the wealthy woman who had employed him as her personal priest. After his death, he reportedly continued to visit his mistresses and even the wealthy elderly woman, feasting on their blood freely. It was said that the monks in Melrose Abbey dragged him from his tomb and set him on fire. But this is evidently not the case because he is alive and well too. And he is the reason I am here. He seems to have a grudge against your people, Sister Joan Phillippe. I came to warn you."

"1196! That makes this Hunderprest even older than Dracula!" Father Gallagher's face looked decidedly green.

"I've been hunting vampires for—" Sister Joan Phillippe caught herself abruptly, looked at the men standing around her like sentinels and frowned. "Well, for a very long time. Why now? Why is he suddenly angry with me now?"

"It's not just you," Phillippe said. "He's after some woman named Wilhelmina Harker."

"Mina!" They all cried her name at once.

"You do know this person? You can warn her?" Phillippe was instantly alert again, watching each face.

"You must go, Michael," Sister Joan Phillippe said, clutching his arm. "She has no idea! And her last letter… I just know she is in great danger in America."

"America!" Phillippe swore and began to pace the room, his massive feet making the space seem even smaller. "That country is crawling with vampires! The war they just fought made it a veritable feast for these creatures. Do you know what you'll be walking into?"

"We have to go," Van Helsing said. "She will need our help."

"What if Hunderprest comes here while we're gone, Sister?" Father Gallagher's eyes wore that haunted look she remembered from his childhood.

"You are not my protector, Michael," she reminded him gently. "God is. And He was performing the job long before you came along. I'll be fine. Go to Mina. She's going to need your help."

He nodded, genuflecting over her and praying with all his heart that she would be safe in his absence.

"What about you, my friend? What will you do now?" Sister Joan Phillippe's words to the large stranger stopped them all. They turned to wait for his answer.

"You were the one who taught me to listen for God's voice," he said. "Everything within me wants to stay here and protect you. But that Voice is telling me to go with them." He looked at Father Gallagher and Van Helsing and hesitated. "If you'll allow me to."

"I'll make the travel arrangements," Van Helsing said. "I have a feeling our friend, Lord Holmwood will want to join the party. And perhaps he can help with the tickets too."

"I'll pack and fill Father Matthew in on the details," Father Gallagher said.

"We'll meet back here, *ya*?" Van Helsing said, bowing toward Phillippe before he exited with Father Gallagher on his heels.

"You have the strangest friends, Sister," Phillippe murmured under his breath. She laughed and motioned toward the chairs by the fireplace.

"Let's sit and chat for a while," Sister Joan Phillippe said gently. "I want to hear all about your journey and about the Voice of God you've been hearing, my friend. Who knows when we'll have a chance to visit like this again? It will take some time to make all the arrangements, but they won't leave without you. I promise."

A startled squeak told her that Sister Martina had returned unexpectedly.

"You may bring us tea for two now, Sister," she said with a smile. Phillippe chuckled softly as the little nun scurried from the room.

To be continued in Mina: Book 2

MEET THE AUTHORS

Jim Doran is a genre writer who enjoys transporting his readers into worlds of wonder, mystery, and danger. Whether it's the fairytale hijinks in the five novels of his Kingdom Fantasy series or his multi-genre short stories, Jim aims to entertain his audience with every word. He's been published in Havok, Every Day Fiction, and the *Moonlight and Claws* and *Casting Call* anthologies. When he's not writing, he's usually enjoying the seasons in Michigan or playing a board game.

Kaitlyn Emery started her career at a young age, winning a multi-district school writing project in the wake of 9/11 to help kids cope with the state of the world around them. Her writing journey was based in the harsh truth that reality was darker than fiction. That theme would become an anthem in her life, following her into adulthood where she channeled her talents to give a voice to the hurting and voiceless, focusing on broken characters people could identify with and often incorporating her love of fantasy to accomplish that goal. Kaitlyn has been featured in various magazines, flash fiction for Havok Publishing, and has had stories published in several anthologies including *Rebirth, Sensational, Prismatic, Casting Call, When Your Beauty is the Beast, Tales from the Tower, Moonlight and Claws, The Depths We'll Go To, The Heights We'll Fly To, Aphotic Love, Fool's Honor, Sharper Than Thorns, Masquerade, Animal Kingdom* (Fall 2022), and a Valentine's Day themed anthology coming out in 2023 (title unreleased). For more information, you can visit her website at www.Kaitlyn-Emery.com or follow her on Instagram under @kaitlyn_scribbling where she is addicted to getting the perfect bookstagram aesthetic!

Believing firmly in magic and merriment, valor and peace, and that sometimes the light shines brightest in the dark places, **Abigail**

Falanga is an author of fantasy and science fiction and possibly is a fairy. She lives in New Mexico with family, books, too many hobbies, and wild ambitions that frequently get out of hand. With an addiction to writing flash fiction and short stories published in various anthologies, Abigail has also published a book and is the co-editor of the *Whitstead Anthologies*.

Pam Halter is a children's book author and editor. Her picture book series, Willoughby and Friends (Fruitbearer Publishing,) have won Purple Dragonfly awards and a Realm Award. The latest release for Willoughby is a coloring/activity book. Pam had fun working hands-on alongside her publisher for that. She also published a YA fantasy, *Fairyeater*, (Love2ReadLove2Write Publishing), which is also a recipient of a Purple Dragonfly. Her short stories appear in several anthologies, including the *Whitstead* books and *Realmscapes*, as well as Ye Olde Dragon Books. Pam lives in South Jersey where she enjoys writing, gardening, cooking, quilting and playing the piano. She enjoys walking on long country roads where she finds fairy homes, emerging dragons, and trees eating wood gnomes. Learn more about her at *www.pamhalter.com*.

On the road to publication, **Michelle Levigne** fell into fandom in college and has 40+ stories in fanzines in various SF and fantasy universes. She has a bunch of useless degrees in theater, English, film/communication, and writing. Even worse, she has over 100 books and novellas with multiple small presses, in science fiction and fantasy, YA, suspense, women's fiction, and sub-genres of romance. Her training includes the Institute for Children's Literature; proofreading at an advertising agency; and working at a community newspaper. She is a tea snob and freelance edits for a living. (*MichelleLevigne@gmail.com* for info/rates), but only enough to give her time to write. Her newest crime against the literary world is to be co-managing editor at Mt. Zion Ridge Press and launching the publishing co-op, Ye Olde Dragon Books. Be afraid… be very afraid.

Lindsi McIntyre is a linguaphile from Texas who hopes to use her words, both written and spoken, to bring glory to the Lord Most High. When not writing she can be found within the pages of a good book, or watching the latest episode of her favorite TV shows, and drinking way too much tea while doing both. You can check out more of her work on Havok, grab a copy of *Moonlight and Claws* and *Tales from the Tower* anthologies from Ye Olde Dragon books, and look for her award-winning novella *Broken Pieces* on Amazon.

Stoney M. Setzer lives south of Atlanta, GA. He has a beautiful wife, three wonderful children, and one crazy dog, and he is also a diehard Atlanta Braves fan. He has written a trilogy of novels about small-town amateur sleuth Wesley Winter (*Dead of Winter*, *Valley of the Shadow*, and *Day of Reckoning*). In October 2022, he is re-releasing his short story anthology *Zero Hour*, featuring Twilight Zone-like stories with Christian themes. Mr. Setzer is currently writing a novel centering on the fictional community of Sardis County, Tennessee. His previous contributions to the Ye Olde Dragons anthologies are part of this series. He has also written historical fiction stories about Zacchaeus, Samson, and Barabbas for Faith Journeys app, available on your app store. Learn more at *www.tinniepress.blogspot.com* or on Facebook@ stoneymsetzerofficial.

Deborah Cullins Smith participated in several anthologies before publishing back-to-back releases of her Last of the Long-Haired Hippies trilogy--*Shroud of Darkness*, *The Birth of the Storm*, and *Victoria's War*, all with CWG Press. Her newest series is a remake of the Mina Harker legend, beginning with *Mina: Warrior in the Shadows*, released December 2021, and won the Realm Award for Best Horror Novel of 2022. She also has stories in the anthologies *When Your Beauty Is the Beast*, *Moonlight and Claws*, *Tales from the Tower* and *Two Olde Dragons Writing Wyrd Stories*. Deborah is co-editor and partner in Ye Olde Dragons Books. She is also the grandmother of fourteen and loves nothing more than a rousing tea party with a table full of children. When she isn't writing, she can generally be found watching movies and knitting, while curled up with her chihuahua, Lulu. Your best chance of finding her is at the Ye Olde Dragon Fiction Fan Group on Facebook.

C.S. (Chris) Wachter lives in rural Lancaster County, Pennsylvania, with her husband, two dogs and two cats. They have been married for more than forty years and have three sons, one grandson and one granddaughter. She started writing when she retired in 2015. In 2018 she published the four books of *The Seven Words Epic Fantasy* series, followed in 2019 by a short story and sequel continuing the Seven Words story. The first book in the series, *The Sorcerer's Bane*, won Indies Today 2020 Award in the Religion category. In 2020 she published the *Stone Sovereigns* YA Fantasy duology. In 2021, two of her short stories were included in the anthologies, *When Your Beauty is the Beast* and *Moonlight and Claws*. She has also written various flash fiction pieces for Havok. She can be found at *https://cswachter.com/*

Raised in a family obsessed with science fiction, fantasy, and role-play, it was only a matter of time before **Etta-Tamara Wilson** began trying her hand at her own stories. A childhood spent haunting the forests, villages, castles and abbeys of Central Europe resulted in a deep-seated fascination with the original forms of fairy tales, especially the rarely told ones. She's now deep in negotiations with a myriad of fairy tale characters, reminding them to mind their manners and be patient while she works out plotlines and determines who to write about first. She looks forward to seeing who ends up making it to the finish line first: Rumplestiltskin, the Pied Piper, Puss-in-Boots, the Big Bad Wolf, or the twins of the Juniper Tree. Her previous story *Blood Gold* can be found in the *Tales from the Tower* anthology.

Thanks for reading!

We hope you enjoyed this new volume of Classic Monster retellings and re-imaginings – and as we say quite often, "turning the trope on its ear!"

If you enjoyed this anthology, would you do us a favor and go to Goodreads, or other book review sites, like on whatever online store where you bought this book, and leave a review? We'd appreciate it greatly!

Don't leave yet!

Coming in 2023 – Fairytale Anthology #3: PERCHANCE TO DREAM

Where we take the story of Sleeping Beauty and …. Turn it on its ear!

Please check back, visit our blog, browse our online store, and see what other fun, strange, silly, intriguing and just plain wyrd stories you might enjoy reading!

www.YeOldeDragonBooks.com

Two Olde Dragons Writing Wyrd Stories ….

For YOU!